I0591445

LUNAR CRISIS

SHADOW VANGUARD, BOOK TWO

TOM DUBLIN

MICHAEL ANDERLE

DISRUPTIVE IMAGINATION

LMBPN Publishing
PMB 196, 2540 South Maryland Pkwy
Las Vegas, NV 89109

First Edition, June 2018

LUNAR CRISIS TEAM

JIT Beta Readers -
From all of us, our deepest gratitude!

James Caplan
Micky Cocker
John Ashmore
Kim Boyer
Paul Westman

*If we missed anyone, **please** let us know!*

Damkin Prime, City of Loturn, Back Street Slave Market

Adina Choudhury dialed her modified Jean Dukes Special up to five, aimed the weapon at the forehead of the auctioneer in the center of the abandoned warehouse, and fired.

The Huttut's head exploded in a mass of blood, bone fragments, and brain tissue, showering the stunned crowd with a mixture of all three.

Panic quickly overruled any sense of satisfaction caused by the illegal sale of chained alien children and the customers ran for cover.

"Nice shooting!" enthused Tc'aarlat through Adina's earpiece. "He won't be selling kids again any time soon. Score one for the Shadows!"

"Thanks," replied Adina, sweeping her gun to the left and awarding the biggest-spending slave buyer a two-inch-wide hole through his chest and heart. "A little messier than I'd originally planned, but effective all the same."

"Not as messy as this, though," promised Tc'aarlat. "See the Huttut with the green shirt running for the north-west exit?"

"Yeah..."

WHUMPH!

A blueish-white beam of charged atoms screamed across the warehouse from a platform to Adina's right, slicing through the target's throat and almost decapitating him.

The slave dealer's head wobbled at a disturbing angle for a few seconds before the heavy-set alien fell to his knees, then face-first to the floor.

A fleeing Shrillexian caught the side of the dealer's blood-soaked cranium with his foot as he ran for the exit, severing the few remaining tendons keeping it attached to its owner's body.

The kick caused the now-detached head to roll across the stained concrete floor and straight into an overturned bucket.

"GOOOOAAAALLLL!" roared Tc'aarlat into his headset.

SKAWWWWW! shrieked the raal hawk perched on his shoulder.

"Keep your voice down!" hissed Jack Marber over the private comm channel. "And that goes for Mist as well!"

"Yes, but did you see that!" Tc'aarlat exclaimed.

Despite his desire to keep control of the situation, Jack smiled. "Yes, I saw that, and that's the last time I'm letting you watch my recording of the 1966 soccer World Cup final!"

"What? Why?"

"You may remember that England beat Germany 4-2 without resorting to kicking the opposing team's heads around."

"You're just a sore loser!" Tc'aarlat teased.

"Sore loser?" Jack protested, turning the dial of his own weapon from the infamous labs of Jean Dukes up to a solid six. "OK, I'll see your 'goal' and raise you this..."

K-THUNK!

Both Tc'aarlat and Adina peered out from their respective hiding places and watched as a single black puck about half an inch wide shot across the warehouse. It blasted through the left eye of a Skaine money-lender, exited through the back of his skull, slammed into the mouth of a furious gray alien standing behind him, shattering her teeth, and killing her instantly.

"Bravo!" cried Tc'aarlat, setting his weapon down so he could applaud the shot. "I'm big enough to admit when I'm beaten. The last piece of chocolate cake in the ship's galley is yours."

"Much appreciated," muttered Jack, flicking the dial of his gun up another notch and drawing a bead on the owner of the warehouse as he dashed for his reinforced office and the chance of living to sell children another day.

But Jack wasn't going to allow that to happen.

"Last one to rupture a bad guy's spleen buys the coffee."

ICS *Fortitude*, **Bridge**

"We are ready for departure," announced Solo, the vast cargo ship's Entity Intelligence. "Please fasten your safety belts in preparation for take-off."

Jack spun in the pilot's seat and flicked a withering glance at the digitized face of the middle-aged woman floating on the viewscreen in front of him.

"Really?" he demanded. "Are you going to insist we turn off all electronic items and lift our seat trays into a locked and upright position as well?"

"Actually, Captain Marber, that's a very good—"

"It was a joke, Solo!" Jack exclaimed. "Please just get us in the air."

"Not until all safety belts have been securely fastened."

Jack closed his eyes and worked to calm his breathing. "Yes, Solo," he agreed through clenched teeth.

Dragging his seatbelt across his chest, he slotted the metal end of the strap into its buckle, ensuring the EI was able to hear the satisfying CLICK!

"There!" he exclaimed pointedly. "Happy?"

"I am incapable of experiencing biological emotions such as happiness, Captain," Solo replied. "But as a close approximation, I am now sufficiently satisfied with your compliance with safety regulations that I am prepared to continue with our scheduled maneuver."

Jack turned to face the ship's controls and tapped a command into the keyboard embedded in the ancient-looking racks of equipment. "I've really got to get Adina to take a close look at your core programming," he muttered.

"You've got to get me to do what?" inquired Adina as she stepped onto the bridge.

"Delve into the programming of Bossy Knickers up

there," Jack said. "She's off on one of her smothering sessions again."

Adina chuckled. "I actually don't mind that she goes the extra mile to look after us," she admitted. "Then again, she doesn't look like *my* mother."

"I told you, that was not my decision!" Jack blustered. "Solo went into my service history without my permission."

"Good morning, Adina," Solo interrupted. "Please would you be so kind as to secure your safety belt so that I may proceed with lift-off?"

"Of course, Solo!" beamed Adina, slotting the buckle of her seatbelt into place. "I'm more than happy to do so."

"Thank you, Adina." The EI smiled. "It is refreshing that at least one of the crew members understands the need to follow the former Empire's strict safety regulations."

"Teacher's pet!" grumbled Jack under his breath.

"Where's Tc'aarlat?" asked Adina, gesturing to the empty copilot's seat.

"Checking on the kids to make sure they're ready to leave," Jack replied. "He said some of them are a little nervous. The slave traders kidnapped them when they were very young, and they don't remember much if anything about the families coming to collect them when we land."

"Understandable," agreed Adina. "They've been through a lot. Imagine watching your friends and siblings being sold off to work as unpaid servants for unscrupulous toffs or to fill the bellies of cannibalistic merchants."

Jack shook his head slowly and stared into the distance.

"It's a shitty way to live, if you can even call it living. At least some of them will make it home."

"There'll be more out there," Adina offered. "We may have closed down the slave ring here, but whoever that Huttut was working for is bound to have other kids elsewhere. Those types don't put all their eggs in one basket."

"Who's a bastard?" asked Tc'aarlat, entering the bridge and heading for his seat. On his leather shoulder pad, Mist was busy preening her deep-red feathers.

Adina rolled her eyes. "Not 'bastard,' 'basket!'"

The Yollin shrugged, his mandibles spreading wide. "OK then, who's a basket?"

"Snel Gardlarr, that turd-faced slave trader we just fucked up," answered Jack. "I had Solo download all the contacts and messages from his tablet and send them to Nathan. Hopefully he'll get Christina and Terry Henry to track some of those fuckers down and we'll find out just how deep the rabbit hole goes."

Tc'aarlat sat back in his chair, confused. "Baskets? Rabbit holes? It's no wonder I can never keep up with conversations around here. You humans have weird ways of saying shit. You don't say what you mean."

"Well, don't try to join in then," warned Jack. "I don't want to have to follow you around apologizing every time you inform someone that 'the penis is mightier than the sword.'"

"Hey, that phrasebook had very small writing!" protested Tc'aarlat, reaching into a nearby dish of cubed meat and plucking a piece out to feed to Mist. "And I'm pretty sure they weren't real nuns either."

The trio fell silent. For a few minutes, the only noises

on the bridge were the distant hum of the ship's engines and Mist tearing into her chunk of muri.

"Why haven't we taken off yet?" Tc'aarlat asked, looking at the avatar of Solo on the forward viewscreen. The EI was doing her very best to look aloof and avoid his gaze.

"Seatbelt," said Adina and Jack in unison.

"For fuck's sake!" grumbled the Yollin as he reached for his safety harness. "Are we still letting this jumped-up toaster oven push us around?"

Jack gave him a wry smile. "Just try to remember that that 'toaster oven' can easily cut off our oxygen supply if she doesn't like what you say about her."

"Fair point," Tc'aarlat acknowledged quietly. "Thank you for your concern, Solo," he told the EI pleasantly as he secured his harness. "I feel safer already."

"I'm so glad," said Solo, finally sending the command to take off to the necessary ship's components. "Now please sit back and enjoy the flight."

The Yollin folded his arms. "Don't you worry about that," he responded, wiggling around to get as comfortable as possible. "I've been awake for forty-eight hours straight. Nothing's going to stop me from relaxing for the next week at the very least."

The ICS *Fortitude* rose gently into the air. The run-down warehouse buildings, crumbling homes, and hideaways for people traffickers and drug addicts across Loturn City fell away, soon disappearing from view as the ship passed through the cloud layer and continued to rise into the lower atmosphere.

"That's what I'm talking about!" Tc'aarlat sighed happily, closed his eyes, and settled down for the flight.

Exactly six seconds later alarms shrieked from every speaker, screen, and tablet on the bridge.

Tc'aarlat's eyes shot capital-O wide. "What the fuck?!"

Jack spun in his chair. "Solo, report!"

The EI's face returned to the screen. "We have incoming, Captain."

"'Incoming?'" spat Tc'aarlat. "Incoming *what*? An incoming video call? Incoming mail? Is someone trying to deliver a pepperoni pizza?"

Solo shook her head. "My apologies, Tc'aarlat. I should have been more precise. We have an incoming missile."

"What? Who the fuck fired that at us?" Jack barked.

"I do not currently have that information," replied Solo, "although I am scanning the schematics of the missile for clues to narrow down the identity of the aggrieved party."

Tc'aarlat gripped the sides of his seat, silently pleased he was wearing his safety harness. "Aggrieved party? I'd say we've gone a tiny bit further than 'aggrieved' if these Bistok-frotters are trying to blow us out of the sky!"

Adina unclipped her seatbelt and jumped to her feet.

"Please return to your position and fasten your safety belt, Adina," Solo told her firmly.

"No can do!" yelled Adina in reply as she raced for the door leading off the bridge. "Those kids back there will be terrified. They need someone with them."

She disappeared into the dimly-lit corridor and the sound of her feet pounding on the metal floor quickly faded.

The ship banked hard to starboard, and through the forward viewscreen Jack and Tc'aarlat saw a sleek red missile shoot past them, a thick contrail spewing from its engine.

"I took the liberty of implementing evasive maneuvers, Captain," Solo admitted. "I trust that was not too bold a decision on my part."

"No!" snapped Jack, flicking switches to activate the external cameras. "Keep taking liberties!"

"Thank you for your confidence," replied Solo with a smile. "Now please remain seated. A second projectile is heading our way."

"Then what are you waiting for?" cried Jack. "Take evasive maneuvers again!"

"I'm afraid that is not an option this time."

"Why the fuck not?"

Solo's avatar sighed. "Because this second missile is enhanced with heat-seeking technology...

"And it has just locked on."

2

Planet Taglen, Lymak City, Temple of Persha

High Priest Jolio Phisk adjusted the golden robes around his shoulders, then raised both hands in the air, palms upward, as he prayed.

Seated on scores of long wooden benches, almost two thousand pious worshippers copied their leader's posture.

"Venerable Goddess Persha..." began Phisk, the tiny microphone clipped to his vestments causing his voice to boom from the powerful speakers placed around the lavish church. "We your loyal servants request your divine judgment for our thoughts and actions."

On cue, the congregation's deferential voices responded aloud, "Judge us, beloved Goddess."

Phisk lowered his hands and rested them on the white-marbled surface of the altar before him.

"Goddess Persha, we thank you for laying down the three laws which govern our society and determine our behavior..."

"We thank you," chanted the crowd in return.

The high priest raised his eyes to the ceiling and continued.

"You shall obey all decrees from the Goddess Persha."

"We shall obey," intoned the congregation.

"We shall not violate any blessed decree."

"We shall not violate."

"We shall condemn those who defy any blessed decree."

"We shall condemn."

"For it is only by obeying each and every decree shall you be judged pure enough to ascend into the company of Hann, twin sister of Persha and Goddess of Eternal Pleasure."

"Blessed is the Goddess Hann."

"Let us demonstrate our adoration for Persha and Hann by donating to the temple fund for the clergy's ongoing work with those less fortunate than ourselves," directed Phisk.

As he spoke, wardens in plain white robes stepped out from behind pillars and through arched wooden doors in the temple walls. Each carried a golden tray about the size of a book.

Each warden stood at the end of a bench and passed the tray to the person sitting next to the aisle. On cue, the first worshipper produced a plastic card from their pocket and laid it on the tray. There was a barely-audible *beep* as the card's data chip was read and a pre-determined monetary donation was withdrawn from the user's bank account. The tray was then passed to the next parishioner.

Before long, the temple was awash with *beeps*. After a few moments the golden platters reached the far ends of the benches, where more wardens were waiting to retrieve them and spirit the digital collections away.

Jolio Phisk waited until the room fell silent, then swept the congregation with an accusing stare.

"All present here today are thankful for the Goddess Persha's constant presence in our lives and of the joyous judgment she so gracefully bestows upon us."

The faithful bowed their heads as one.

The High Priest paused for a second before continuing in a darker, more malevolent tone. "She is aware that there are sinners among us. She is ready to judge."

Heads remained bowed throughout the temple.

"Let those who can identify a sinner speak now, on pain of punishment."

Swiftly, the entire congregation lifted their heads and looked around the room, studying loved ones and strangers alike.

Hushed whispers and quietly muttered conversations echoed from the vaulted ceiling high above.

Then, slowly and hesitantly, a man in the fourth row raised his hand. He cleared his throat and spoke as if reluctantly revealing some precious secret. "My wife..."

He paused to throw a brief glance toward the suddenly horrified woman on his left. "My wife took the Goddess Persha's name in vain when she forgot to check on the dinner she was cooking and everything burned."

A collective gasp rose around the temple. The worshippers were very aware of the punishment for cursing with either deity's name.

"Bring her forward," Phisk commanded.

Blinking away the sweat dripping into his eyes from his

forehead, the man grabbed his wife's hand and pulled her to her feet.

"No, Corlon, please! No!" she begged as people farther along the pew tucked in their legs to allow the couple to pass. "Please, Corlon. You know I didn't mean it. I was just disappointed I'd ruined our special meal, is all. I love you, sweetheart."

After dragging his wife into the aisle, the man glanced at Jolio Phisk. When he turned back to face his wife, his expression had changed. It was softer, more loving, and full of regret.

"Merfel," he said, "I can't—"

"Bring her forward!" Phisk repeated.

Nodding, Corlon found his confidence once more. He tightened his grip on his wife's wrist and led her up to the front of the temple. There she sank to her knees, tears streaming down her face.

Her husband released his grip and stepped back a few paces, leaving his wife to face Persha's glorious judgment alone.

"Name?" demanded the High Priest.

"M-merfel Strumm," stammered the woman. "But Corlon—my husband—he's wrong, sir. I really didn't—"

"Silence!"

"Did you take the Goddess Persha's name in vain?"

"Please, sir, I was only—"

"Did you take the Goddess's name in vain, yes or no?"

"Yes, but—"

"Then I shall pray for you."

Phisk closed his eyes and lifted his face to the ceiling. "Glorious Persha, gift this unworthy disciple, Merfel

Strumm, with your divine judgment through me, your humble servant."

Merfel gazed at the High Priest through her tears, trying hard to ignore her husband's sobs from behind her.

After a moment, Jolio Phisk opened his eyes again and looked down at the terrified woman. "The Goddess Persha has spoken."

The congregation held its collective breath.

"She has kindly judged that you are to be delivered to her sister, the Goddess Hann," finished Phisk as he withdrew a long golden knife from beneath his robes. The blade glinted in the sunlight streaming through the high stained-glass windows.

"NO!" screamed Merfel. "Please, no!"

Phisk was unmoved by her desperate cries for mercy. "Take the Dagger of Hann!" he commanded, flipping the knife in the air and deftly catching the blade between his fingertips.

The woman stretched up a hand and grasped the cold metal handle with trembling fingers.

Merfel Strumm looked at the High Priest for further instruction, although as a regular churchgoer she already knew what she had to do.

All Jolio Phisk had to say was, "You have been judged."

Nodding, Merfel wiped away her tears with the back of her hand and tore open the front of her shirt, the buttons audibly scattering across the marble floor in the imposing silence of the temple.

She tugged the shirt from her shoulders, baring her ample breasts. Then, pressing the tip of the dagger over the upper left side of her chest, she spoke out loud.

"I offer my thanks to the great Goddess Persha for my holy judgment and entrust my soul to the Goddess Hann and unbridled pleasure for all eternity."

She plunged the dagger deep into her heart.

"NO!" cried Corlon Strumm, but it was too late.

Jolio Phisk watched as the sinner before him fell to her side, the knife still protruding from her chest, her heavy right breast almost obscuring the handle.

Two more wardens dashed out of a side door and grabbed the dead woman beneath her arms. Without a word, they dragged her across the polished stone floor and back toward the room from which they had appeared.

Jolio Phisk didn't look at them or even glance at where concerned parishioners were doing their best to console Corlon Strumm. His body was wracked with violent, harrowing sobs.

"The service is at an end," Phisk pronounced, holding his hands high in the air, palms forward. "Go forth from this place and spread the word that all shall be judged and endure eternal pleasure in the company of the Goddess Hann.

"This is the proclamation of Persha."

"Blessed is the Goddess Persha," responded the congregation, then they began to gather their belongings and ready themselves to leave the temple.

The High Priest watched his flock for a moment, then, with a bow toward the altar, he stepped down from the raised platform and made for the side exit. He took care not to tread in the still-moist trail of blood.

Once inside the room, Phisk removed his robes and

hung them on the closest of a row of hooks attached to the wall.

Turning, he looked down at the body of Merfel Strumm. The female lay on her back in a plain wooden casket, the golden dagger still embedded in her chest.

"Do you think she really did it?" asked a voice. "Did she blaspheme?"

Phisk looked up to find his deputy Dabriel Yagash standing before him. The shorter man was holding a small and ornate golden casket in his hands, its heavily-decorated lid open.

"Who knows?" replied Phisk with a shrug. He gripped the handle of the knife and pulled it free with a visceral *schlupp*. "Her husband said she did."

He handed the weapon to Dabriel, who winced as he took it. Placing it carefully inside the casket without cleaning the blade, he closed the lid and set the golden box aside.

Turning back, his eyes flicked toward the female's corpse, his expression grim.

"How did we do with today's donations?" Phisk asked, pulling Dabriel from his reverie.

Dabriel snatched the top tray from a large stack beneath the window and produced a card similar to those used by the worshippers. He pressed it to the metallic surface.

After a *beep*, the surface of the tray rippled like a still pond after a stone was dropped into it. A number written in swirling black figures shimmered into view as the disturbance calmed.

Dabriel raised his eyebrows. "Very well indeed, sire.

120,307 credits from today's service alone. That makes just under half a million credits overall this past week."

Phisk produced a card of his own from the inside pocket of his jacket and held it out.

"Sire," began Dabriel, "I must protest. You can't really expect me to—"

"I do believe the seasons are changing," interrupted the High Priest, locking eyes with his subordinate. "Which means young Hamble's birthday is approaching, does it not?"

An icy chill ran through Dabriel. "Indeed, your worship."

"How old will she be this time around? Six years old? Seven?"

"Eight, sire." Dabriel's mouth was suddenly dry.

"Eight!" exclaimed Phisk. "My goodness, Dabriel. How quickly they grow. We must pray to the Goddess Persha for her protection, mustn't we?" He waved the card at his subordinate.

"Yes, sire," said Dabriel with a deep sigh. "We must."

Taking the card, he pressed it against the tray. After another *beep* the figure on display was zero.

"May I inquire what your plan is for this money, your worship?" asked Dabriel. "I know there is good work being done in the township of Forlium, where volunteers are building a new shelter for the homeless. And, of course, the city's soup kitchens are in dire need of a cash injection."

Jolio Phisk nodded. "Both very worthy causes."

"Indeed, sire."

"Please offer both charities my best wishes in finding a donor," Phisk told him, holding his hand out for the card.

"Of course, sire." Dabriel tried to hide his disappointment as he laid the card on Phisk's waiting palm. "And where may I contact you, should they respond to your kind words?"

The High Priest tucked the card into his pocket and reached for an expensive overcoat and hat hanging beside his church vestments. "Today's distressing events have left me spiritually drained," he replied, making for a door marked PRIVATE at the back of the room. "I shall need time to reflect and pray to the Goddess for her divine guidance."

"Indeed, your worship."

Phisk nodded. "I'll be on the Moon of Hann, at the Blue Diamond Casino."

Dabriel lowered his eyes. "Of course, sire."

The High Priest paused in the doorway to glance at the corpse of Merfel Strumm. "And ship that thing to the usual place, will you? I want it gone by the time I return."

Moon of Persha, Highway B78

Trace Byrn sat in the back seat of the taxi and watched the desolate gray landscape rush by. She checked her watch for the third time in as many minutes, confirming what she already knew.

In fifteen minutes' time she would be arriving at the gates of the maximum-security prison.

This was the first time she had visited the Moon of Persha. In fact she'd only been off-world once, when her school class had taken a trip to a nature preserve on the moon's sister satellite.

TOM DUBLIN & MICHAEL ANDERLE

Today's excursion was for a very different reason indeed. Trace was here to meet her fiancé for the very first time.

She had found Vimor Malfic through a lonely-hearts ad in the back of her favorite celebrity gossip magazine. The ad had been placed in a section where convicted felons could request letters and gifts from pen pals across the planet.

Trace always scanned the ads, laughing as she pictured the type of sad, lonely reader who would be desperate enough to strike up a friendship—and possibly more—with someone locked up in a jail cell.

And then she'd seen his photograph.

She could tell he was big, even from a poorly-printed black-and-white snapshot taken from the chest up. His forearms bulged against the taut material of his regulation prison shirt, shoulders too wide to be contained within the pulse-quickening image.

Thick curled hair hung around his face, the dark tresses almost begging to have her perfectly manicured fingers brush through them. Due to the low resolution of the grainy image it was difficult to tell where his hair ended and the beard began, not that she really cared that much.

Not since she had looked into those eyes.

They should have been as dark and brooding as the rest of his funereal features, but instead they were pale pools of perfectly pure pleasure. She imagined they were a bright vivid blue, as sparkling as they were clear. They threatened to hypnotize her. To burn deep into her soul, capture her heart, and devour it whole.

And she *wanted* to be devoured.

Her first letter in response to the ad had been short and guarded. He had requested friendship with a view to something more, so she had been friendly. She'd told him a little about herself: where she had grown up, what she did for a living, and what she liked to do in her spare time…but then her writing had stalled.

What could she possibly ask Malfic about? Her research told her that he had been convicted on five counts of first degree murder and sentenced to life imprisonment without parole.

If Taglen hadn't repealed the death sentence a decade earlier, he would now be providing nutrients for the trees growing among the unmarked graves in the prison cemetery located on the uninhabited side of the moon.

She couldn't inquire after his career or hobbies, and she certainly didn't want to ask about his past—although there was a nagging voice at the back of her mind that wanted to know every gory detail about the crimes he had committed.

Shaking herself free of such despicable desires, she had asked after his health, whether he enjoyed reading and what his favorite books were, and how often he managed to get outside and enjoy the fresh air.

His reply had been swift and wonderful. Vimor Malfic's letters were long, detailed, and crafted to provoke feelings of boundless hope and love in ways she could never have imagined.

He was a poet.

Trace had read his beautiful words over and over and her heart had soared. He had sent her a photograph to replace the coarse image she had clipped from the magazine, and yes, his eyes *were* blue—a brilliant sapphire blue that caused her to hear the angels sing.

She had written to him again and again, tucking pictures of her own into the envelopes before mailing her missives to the penitentiary. She had included several she had taken with the help of a timer, rose petals and revealing lingerie.

She knew the guards would check each letter as they arrived, but she didn't care. Let them get a few moments of titillation from her snapshots. All that mattered was that they safely reached her mighty man.

After almost three months of sensuous correspondence, the moment she had been waiting for arrived. Vimor's latest letter had asked if she would visit him in prison after doing him a small favor.

She had danced around her apartment at that, letter clutched to her chest as she tried to imagine that first embrace. The feeling as his big, thick arms wrapped around her slender frame.

Trace had replied the very same day. Of course she would visit, she had promised. And, as for the favor, she would do anything for her guy. Anything at all. It would be her pleasure.

She had to admit that she had been taken aback when Malfic's next love note had detailed how she could find the illegal backstreet chip manufacturer who could manufacture what he needed.

3

ICS Fortitude, Bridge

Jack clung to the sides of his seat while the *Fortitude* banked hard to the right . There was a clearly audible *hisssss* as the heat-seeking rocket on the tail sped by, becoming visible on the forward viewscreens as it turned in the air for a second try at destroying them.

"Solo!" shouted Jack over the noise of the ship's bow-thrusters working overtime. "What are the odds of us avoiding this twatting rocket?"

Her face appeared on the screens around the bridge. "The odds, Captain Marber?" she asked with a frown. "Isn't this an inopportune moment to take up gambling?"

"I meant the scientific odds!" Jack retorted, leaning hard to his right as the ship heeled violently to port to avoid another heat-provoked assault. "I want to know our chances of making it out of this alive!"

"Ah, understood, Captain," Solo responded. "From what I can ascertain, the software controlling the missile is studying our evasive maneuvers and adapting its own movements to try to counter them. As such, I predict our chances are around eighty-two percent."

"That's not bad," Tc'aarlat commented with a dark smile. "An eighty-two percent chance we'll survive is pretty good."

"Oh, I'm sorry," said Solo. "I thought you meant the chances of us being blasted into billions of individual atoms. That is the outcome I was predicting with the figure of eighty-two percent."

Tc'aarlat's eyes grew wide. "You mean the odds of us not dying are *only eighteen percent*?"

"That is correct," replied Solo. "And please accept my congratulations on the speed at which you calculated that figure."

"My brain works faster when it learns it has just two minutes left in one piece!" the Yollin barked.

"That conclusion is, however, incorrect," Solo told him calmly. "We passed the two-minute mark a little over ninety seconds ago."

"We've got thirty *seconds* left to live?" exclaimed Jack. "Why didn't you tell us?"

Solo adopted a serious expression. "I didn't want to worry you, Captain."

Jack ignored the excuse and hit the button that would allow him to talk over the speaker system in the cargo hold. "Adina, get the kids away from the sides of the ship and brace for impact!"

Tc'aarlat snatched Mist from her perch.

SKAWWW!

He clutched the bird tightly to his chest, leaned forward

in an effort to protect her with his exoskeleton, and cried, "Good luck!"

"Thanks!" said Jack from the pilot's seat.

Tc'aarlat glanced in his direction. "Yeah, you too."

This time it was Jack's eyes that widened. "You were talking to your fucking bird?"

"Hey, I've known her a lot longer than—"

Solo's voice interrupted their conversation. "Missile impact in five, four, three—"

A huge explosion rocked the entire ship. Jack and Tc'aarlat covered their heads with their arms as the screams of terrified children echoed along the corridors.

After a moment Jack opened his eyes again. "We made it," he breathed. "We're still alive!"

"Solo!" croaked Tc'aarlat, "what happened? Did the missile hit us?"

"It did not," Solo responded. "My sensors show it was shot out of the air less than a few hundred meters behind our main engines."

"Shot out of the air?" repeated Jack. "Who's responsible for that?"

"That would be me!" announced an unfamiliar voice over the comm. "You can thank me in person once I've docked in your rear hangar bay."

Moon of Hann, Blue Diamond Casino, Card Table Eight

Lowlon Quell tried to steady his nerves as he slid a lime-green chip across the soft felt of the card table toward the waiting croupier.

"Ten thousand credits on twenty-eight," he declared,

fighting to keep his voice from betraying the panic he was feeling. This was by far the biggest bet he'd ever made, and the last thing he wanted was for the other players sitting at the table to realize he was bluffing.

After a sixteen-year career as a semi-professional gambler, Make Twenty-Eight was now his game of choice. Requiring more luck than roulette, more skill than black-jack, and more tactical thinking than poker, Make Twenty-Eight was the game gamblers played when they wanted to claim their winnings were more the result of hard work than just the turn of a card.

And Quell had worked hard at progressing in his career. Certainly harder than he had at his day job as a claims inspector for a small family-owned insurance brokerage back on the planet Taglen below.

His bosses—the husband-and-wife team who had started the business—had put up with his gambling much longer than they should have.

They'd tolerated the large number of days Quell had called in absent following a long weekend at one racetrack or another. The absences were required either because he had a hangover after celebrating his wins or due to the fact that he'd lost every single credit he owned and had no way to get back from the moon.

They'd kept their opinions to themselves when he had requested advances on his paychecks to pay off gambling debts in order to remain the owner of all of his fingers and/or both of his ears.

They had even allowed him extra time to repay the loan they had made to him so that he could spend his vacation in a clinic which specialized in treating those addicted to gambling—a clinic he had been ejected from for taking bets on the order of deaths of the residents of the adjoining care home for the elderly.

The final straw, however, had been when he was out delivering a check to a customer whose house had burned to the ground thanks to an undetected electrical fault. Quell had talked the woman into loaning him the two-hundred-thousand-credit pay-out, promising to return with double the money for each of them since he had a tip on a dead cert in a zero-gravity ultimate fighting tournament being held the following day.

The insurance company had been forced to repay the money he had conned from the victim, and the only reason the owners hadn't reported him to the authorities was that he was keeping up his monthly cash installments to settle the debt.

Lowlon Quell had taken his sudden unemployment as a sign from the twin Goddesses that his day job had just been holding him back. He relocated to the Moon of Hann, moved into a run-down hotel for transients and drifters located in a rough neighborhood far from the bright lights of the casino district, and doubled down on his attempt to win his way to a life of luxury.

And now he had the chance to make that happen, or, at least move into a guest house which wasn't overrun with tiny red-backed insects which infested his sheets and dropped from the ceiling into his food several times per day.

This was his chance to be a real player.

"Do any of you wish to receive extra cards?" the

croupier asked, turning first to one of the three other players at the table.

The male—a Taglenian—rolled two translucent twenty-sided dice the same color as his lavender eyes across his portion of the table, then shook his head without lifting his gaze from the six cards already clutched tightly in his silk-gloved hands.

The next gambler was a female Yollin dressed in a wide-brimmed hat and a fringed jacket studded with rhinestones. Her two silver-plated dice reflected the over-head lights as they tumbled over the green felt, stopping with a six and a nineteen on their upper surfaces.

Seeing the result, she smiled at the croupier. "Two, please."

The dealer slid two cards from the deck and passed them over, face-down. Quell watched the Yollin's expression closely as she studied the additions to her hand but she gave nothing away.

The Malatian sitting next to Quell tossed his pair of mismatched dice forcefully, squinting to see their top-most numbers after they had bounced off the bumper at the croupier's side of the table. He thought for a long moment, then grunted "One." He snatched the offered card and glanced at it, then tossed his entire hand onto the playing surface before grabbing his dice and striding angrily away across the casino floor.

That left Quell competing against just two other partic-ipants, greatly increasing his chances of winning...and winning big.

This development deserved his special dice.

Reaching into his shirt pocket, he produced a small

black velvet bag. Loosening the drawstring, he reverently removed two shimmering yellow twenty-siders, dropping his more basic black-and-white dice inside the bag.

"Wait a second," said the Yollin, her previously kind smile evaporating, "have those dice been tested by the dealers?"

The croupier nodded. "Mr. Quell is a regular player," she confirmed. "He often switches dice mid-game, and both sets have been verified properly."

"Well, all right," drawled the Yollin. "But I'll be watchin' 'em close."

"You're welcome to inspect them yourself," Lowlon Quell offered, holding out the dice.

The female glanced at Quell's hand, then at his face. He could tell she still wasn't happy with this unusual tactic but realized there was little she could do about it. "If this little lady assures us they've been verified it's all right by me."

Offering a smile of thanks, Lowlon closed his fingers around the dice, blew between the digits, and shook the two multi-faceted objects.

Finally he opened his hand and allowed them to fly. He watched as they soared over his cards and bounced once, then twice as they hit the soft table covering.

The dice rolled, numbers appearing and instantly disappearing from view as they gradually slowed. Slower and slower they moved until...

Nine and four.

Quell's eyes lost their focus for a split-second as he made a number of quick mental calculations.

Nine and four. Nine and four. Nine and four.

That meant he needed two extra cards. Added to the

cards already in his possession, a two and a six would almost certainly win him the game, but a pair of sevens...

Persha's blessed ass! A pair of sevens would earn him the jackpot.

A million fucking credits!

Suddenly aware of his pounding heart, Quell looked at the other players and the croupier. They were all staring back at him intently, but as far as he could tell they could neither hear the rapid pounding inside his chest nor see the material of his shirt moving with each heartbeat.

No one else knew he was *this* close to finally achieving the status he had desired and chased for so long now.

He would be a winner.

The things he could do with that many credits! He'd pay off those goody-goody fuckwits at the insurance company for one, then he'd get a better apartment—one within walking distance of—"

"Any extra cards, Mr. Quell?"

His dream-bubble popping, Quell forced himself to focus on the face of the croupier. What was her name again? Milly? Molly? Mandy?

Forget it, Lowlon. It doesn't matter.

"Two," he said as calmly as he could, quickly adding, "Please."

Almost in slow motion, the croupier slid the cards from the deck and handed them over. Quell took them, suddenly wanting to do *anything* other than turn them over and see what they were.

He wanted to run. To hide. To close his eyes and never open them again. If he blew this—the closest he'd ever come to winning this big—he would never be able to forgive himself.

But what if...

"Hurry up!" snapped the female Yollin, all trace of her previously kind expression gone from her features. Now her mandibles were closed across her mouth, tapping out a beat of impatience and frustration.

OK, Lowlon. This is it. Do it.

Just. Fucking. Do it.

Quell turned over the first card and almost cried out.

It was a seven.

If he had gotten another seven he was made for life. Well, maybe not for *life*, but at least for the next year of that life—a year in which he would have nothing more to worry about than winning more credits.

All he had to do was...

He turned the card.

And stared.

It was another seven.

He'd done it.

He'd won the jackpot.

His entire world went black.

Lower Atmosphere of Damkin Prime, ICS *Fortitude*, Rear Cargo Bay

Adina joined Jack and Tc'aarlat just as the captain was pressing his palm against the rear wall of the cargo bay.

"What the hell happened?" she hissed as the wall slid down and disappeared into a hidden compartment beneath their feet and revealed a large, but empty, hangar beyond.

This was the space where, until the conclusion of their first mission, the team had kept a sleek black spacecraft known as the *Pegasus*.

Much to Tc'aarlat's dismay, the *Pegasus* had been destroyed when Solo had rammed it into a tower block in a last-ditch effort to gain access to the only computer they could use to stop an imminent gravity storm instigated by maliciously-coded nanobots.

He still had nightmares about the wreck of twisted metal, torn leather seats, and—worst of all—the broken blue LED lights which had made the interior compartment look really exciting and futuristic.

"Some smarmy show-off shot down the heat-seeking missile on our tail," Tc'aarlat explained. "Now he's invited himself aboard so we can shower him with our thanks."

SKRORRR! shrieked Mist from his shoulder.

Adina fought the urge to smile. "'Smarmy show-off?'"

"Bound to be," replied the Yollin. "You watch, he'll be all 'ooh, look at me, I'm such a sharkshooter!'"

Jack turned, frowning, as the hangar door finally vanished with a metallic CLUNK! "The word is 'sharpshooter,' not 'sharkshooter.'"

"Oh," said Tc'aarlat thoughtfully. "I suppose that makes more sense, and it's far less cruel to sharks."

Shaking his head, Jack turned back to face the hangar. "Open the hangar doors, Solo."

"Yes, Captain Marber." There was a subtle *whoosh*, then the far wall of the hangar split in two and began to open outwards, allowing the trio to see the bright but overcast sky beyond.

Something moved deep within the clouds, then a spaceship eased itself through the swirling whiteness and made for the hangar entrance.

It was a black spaceship.

A sleek black spaceship.

A sleek black spaceship whose pilot was illuminated by the light from dozens of brilliant blue LEDs.

It was an exact copy of the *Pegasus*.

Jack and Adina turned when they heard a heavy *thud* and the sound of Mist's wings pumping hard against the air as she flew up to perch on a steel support.

Tc'aarlat had fainted.

4

Lower Atmosphere of Damkin Prime, ICS _Fortitude_, Rear Hangar

When Tc'aarlat's eyes fluttered open, he had a throbbing pain centered at the back of his skull. Adina was standing over him, dabbing his brow with a damp towel.

"Whoa!" he groaned. "What hit me?"

"The edge of the hangar doorway," Adina replied. "You fell back and hit your head against it when you fainted. Jack helped me carry you to this bench so you had somewhere more comfortable to lie than the floor."

The Yollin tentatively touched the painful spot at the back of his head, wincing as his fingers made contact.

"I'm gonna have a bastard of a headache before long," he muttered. "I can already feel it starting to—"

He quickly sat upright, waving his hands to shoo Adina and her cold compress back a few steps. "Wait! I _fainted_?"

"Like a teenage girl at a pop concert." Adina grinned.

Tc'aarlat shook his head...and instantly regretted doing

so because another wave of pain blossomed from the lump on his skull. "No, you've got it wrong. I don't faint. It must have been something else."

"Like what?" questioned Adina.

"I don't know." Tc'aarlat shrugged. "Perhaps it was my brain reacting to the relief of not being blown to bits by that missile."

"By completely shutting down?"

"The brain is a complex organ, Adina," Tc'aarlat offered. "Who knows exactly what might trigger an unexpected reboot?"

"Triggers like unexpectedly seeing the *Pegasus* again?"

Tc'aarlat leapt to his feet. "That was *real*? I thought I'd dreamt it!"

Before Adina could stop him, the Yollin set off at a run toward the bright light emanating from the open hangar doors.

He dashed into the hangar and skidded to a halt. In the center of the sterile space was an exact replica of the shuttle he had been in when it smashed into an office building on Alma Nine.

"It's true!" he croaked. "The *Pegasus* is back!"

"Actually it's the *Pegasus* Mark Two," said Jack, appearing from the far side of the shuttle. "And we owe it our lives."

Tc'aarlat's mandibles spread wide in confusion. "But how... Why... I mean, who was piloting it?"

"That would be me." A figure stepped into view beside Jack. He was tall, slender, and sported a thick mane of shaggy blond hair. His piercing blue eyes flicked from Jack to Tc'aarlat and back.

"Draven Maynard," he said, walking forward and holding out his hand. "Nathan sent me to deliver this replacement shuttle to you—and I'm suddenly very glad I agreed to take the job."

Tc'aarlat held out his hand to shake the newcomer's, but Draven strode past him to reach Adina, who was standing in the doorway. Gently taking her hand in his, he raised it to his lips and planted a quick but lingering kiss on the back. "And whom do I have the sincere pleasure of addressing?" he asked smoothly.

Adina felt her cheeks began to burn and hoped she wasn't blushing too hard. "Adina." She pulled her hand away and surreptitiously wiped the back of it on the leg of her jeans. "Adina Choudhury."

"I'm delighted to make your acquaintance, Adina Choudhury." Draven flashed a smile almost as bright as the overhead lights. "Nathan said the *Fortitude* had a female navigator, but he didn't tell me quite how stunning she was."

Tc'aarlat turned to exchange a look with Jack, opening his mouth and pretending to plunge two fingers down his throat and vomit.

"Oh, and who is *this* beauty?" continued Draven as Mist flapped into the hangar and landed lightly on Adina's shoulder.

"Hello, you gorgeous thing," Draven crooned, stroking the blood-red feathers covering the raal hawk's chest. Mist gave a soft *cawww* and jumped from Adina's shoulder to the pilot's wrist.

"No, no, no!" Tc'aarlat strode over to Draven and swiftly lifted the raal hawk from her new perch. "Mist isn't good

TOM DUBLIN & MICHAEL ANDERLE

with strangers. I wouldn't want you to get scratched or bitten."

"She seemed fine to me," countered Draven.

"Well, she wasn't," snapped Tc'aarlat. "You don't know her like I do. She was showing clear signs of distress."

"Tell us about the new ship," Jack asked, stepping between the two men before their conversation could get out of hand. "Is it an exact copy of the first *Pegasus*?"

"Pretty much," replied Draven, tossing his head to flick his hair from his eyes. Tc'aarlat heard a hushed moan and turned to scowl at Adina. She was blushing again...hard.

"This ship—*Pegasus 2*—was built from the original blueprints but has a superior weapons system, as you saw when I shot that heat-seeker out of the sky before it could blast your asses to kingdom come."

"That wasn't all due to your skill?" inquired Jack.

"I wish," said Draven. "I'm a solid pilot and a decent shot, but even *I'd* find pinpointing a zigzagging missile a little on the tough side. No, the lion's share of the work was done by the on-board weapons tech."

"That could prove useful," Adina pointed out. "You know, if something like that ever happens again."

"Speaking of which," began Draven. "What was that all about? Who was firing big-ass missiles in your direction?"

"We're not exactly sure," Jack admitted. "We think it may have been someone loyal to the slave trader we rescued a bunch of kids from, but that hasn't been confirmed."

Draven raised an eyebrow. "Kids?"

"Yep," said Tc'aarlat. "We raided a slave auction and sent the bad guys who organized it a message they won't forget.

Or, at least they wouldn't if they still had access to their brains."

"That's awesome!" Draven beamed, raising his hand toward Tc'aarlat for a high-five. The Yollin glanced at it and stuffed his hands into the pockets of his overalls. "You know, I've recently had some training in using force to end sieges. I'd be happy to share some tips with you over a couple of beers."

Tc'aarlat forced a smile. "Thanks for the offer, but I don't think there's much you could say that I don't already know. You don't teach your grandmother to fuck eggs, my lad."

"It's 'suck!'" exclaimed Jack. "'Don't teach your grandmother to *suck* eggs!'"

Tc'aarlat frowned. "Elderly human females go around sucking on eggs? They'll never get proper nourishment that way. No wonder they all look so wrinkled."

Jack shook his head slightly. "Sometimes I don't even know where to begin correcting him."

"So..." Draven clapped his hands together. "Where are these kids?"

"In the center cargo hold," replied Adina. "We figured that was the safest place for them. They were pretty scared."

"Then what say we go cheer them up?" Draven flashed his ice-white smile again. "I have some experience in working with disturbed and anxious children. I may be able to help them feel more at ease."

Adina looked at Jack, who nodded. "OK, I'll take you to meet them."

Draven bowed dramatically. "Lead on, fair lady!"

Fighting her instinct to blush again, Adina giggled and hurried out of the hangar.

As she and Draven disappeared, Jack and Tc'aarlat could hear the blond pilot asking Adina about her dream romantic getaway.

"Seems like a nice guy," remarked Jack.

Tc'aarlat sneered. "If you like that sort of thing."

"Adina seems to be a fan."

The Yollin chuckled darkly. "Poor misguided wench."

"Yeah." Jack clapped Tc'aarlat on the shoulder. "I wouldn't call her that to her face if I were you."

Tc'aarlat opened his mouth to respond but Solo cut him off.

"I'm sorry to interrupt, Captain Marber, but I thought you'd want to know that we are closing on our destination."

"Thank you, Solo," replied Jack. "We'll come straight to the bridge."

He and Tc'aarlat stepped out of the hangar, pausing to close the fake wall.

Tc'aarlat kept his eyes fixed on the new *Pegasus* until the metal barrier blocked it from view.

"Absolutely stunning!" he sighed. "I never thought I'd see anything quite as beautiful again."

"Really?" asked Jack. "I got the impression you didn't really like him."

Tc'aarlat scowled. "What? No, not him! I meant the—" He spotted Jack's smirk and chased him in the direction of the bridge.

Moon of Persha, Maximum Security Prison, Visitor Entrance

Trace Byrn flicked open the third button on her pale blue silk blouse and readjusted her push-up bra to ensure the maximum amount of cleavage was on view. She wanted Vimor to remember his first meeting with her for all the right reasons.

She'd been in the line for security for almost thirty minutes now; the process was going slowly. One by one the inmates' visitors were searched and their identities were double-checked, and any items they had brought with them were confiscated until they were ready to leave.

Which was why she had left her purse in a locker at the shuttleport.

The line moved forward after the person at the front was finally given permission to pass through to the next stage of the security process.

Pulling out a tissue she had tucked into her bra, Trace dabbed her forehead to remove the thin sheen of sweat that coated her skin. She swallowed hard. There was no way the security guards could detect the special gift she had arranged for him. Vimor had assured her that she was safe.

Once their letters had progressed to a more personal level, Vimor had written that there was something he desperately wanted; something the overly-strict prison guards would confiscate on sight if she attempted to carry it through security in plain view.

But he knew exactly how Trace could both acquire and smuggle in the object he desired.

Vimor Malfic wanted a certain computer chip.

Trace didn't understand why, but she was determined to go along with his request. She followed the directions cleverly hidden among his endless proclamations of love and desire.

First she had to travel to the city of Ragin and locate a computer engineer in a rather seedy part of town. Once there, she was to give the computer wiz a set of detailed specifications. She didn't understand them, but he assured her that the backstreet genius would.

He had asked Trace to pay for the chip to be manufactured, insisting he would reimburse her for the cost 'in more ways than one' when they finally met.

Trace had needed a hastily-drawn bubble bath and total privacy to deal with her imagination's reaction to *that* statement.

A week later, she was to return to Ragin and collect a small silver computer chip about the size of a small fingernail.

Then came the strange part.

Vimor asked her to swallow it. It would require plenty of water, but the chip should slip down without causing her any unpleasant side-effects.

Once the chip was safely inside her, she was to travel to the Moon of Persha and visit him. He promised her he had formed a friendship with one of the guards, who would arrange for them to be left completely alone for 'as long as necessary.'

That mental image had provoked another urgent bubble bath.

Trace wasn't entirely sure she could promise to—how could she put it—*produce* the computer chip whilst at the prison, but she had spent the intervening time consuming as much fiber-rich food as she could to ensure the necessary event took place.

The tiny silver gizmo would require a thorough cleaning once it had reappeared, but that was a small price to pay to present the new love of her life with the gift he desired so much.

The line moved forward again. Trace would be the next to pass through the metal detector and she felt her heart begin to pound in her chest.

What would happen if the chip triggered the alarms? Would she be taken aside for a full body cavity search? If so, she hoped the guards wouldn't be too surprised at the scanty lingerie she had purchased especially for this visit.

"Next!"

Forcing herself to remain calm, Trace stepped forward, suddenly aware of the *clack clack clack* of her high heels on the stone floor of the visitor security zone.

If she were going to be caught out for smuggling something inside, it would happen now.

She stepped into the phonebooth-sized metal detector to be scanned.

And nothing happened.

No alarms, no flashing lights, no security personnel shouting and reaching for their sidearms.

Nothing.

"Step forward, miss."

Trace did as she was asked and stood with her legs apart and arms outstretched as a pair of guards conducted a thorough and extremely personal body search.

They found nothing more than the spare tissue tucked

into the left cup of her push-up bra, which they handed back to her without comment.

A moment later she was through.

She'd done it. She had illegally transported contraband through prison security and was on her way at long last to meet the man of her dreams, Vimor Malfic, in the flesh.

She wished she had the time to take a quick bubble bath.

Moon of Hann, Blue Diamond Casino, Manager's Office

"He's coming around."

Lowlon Quell opened his eyes and found himself staring up at a ceiling painted deep maroon.

Wherever he was, it wasn't where he'd been.

"How are you feeling, Mr. Quell?"

"OK, I think..." groaned Lowlon. "What happened?"

"I'm afraid you were taken ill," responded the voice. "Our security personnel were good enough to carry you to my office."

Lowlon blinked hard, trying to identify his surroundings. He was lying on a plush red leather couch in a sumptuous office. On a desk made of some dark polished wood were some papers held down by a very expensive-looking fountain pen.

He forced his eyes to focus on the blurry figures leaning over him. One of them was a smartly-dressed man he didn't recognize, but the other person he did know. She was the croupier who had dealt him the cards that had won him the jackp—

"I won!" he yelled, sitting up quickly but immediately wishing he had stayed flat on his back.

"Indeed you did, Mr. Quell," said the unknown , handing over a glimmering Blue Diamond chip with the casino's logo etched into it. "One million credits, no less. You're a very lucky person."

Quell chuckled. "Luck had nothing to do with it." He accepted the chip and kissed it. "It all came down to years of study and skillful playing."

"You're right, of course," the man agreed. "My apologies."

Lowlon pushed himself onto his elbows. "And you are?"

"Forgive me." The man bowed his head slightly. "I'm Thavo Domp, owner of the Blue Diamond Casino."

This time Quell *did* sit up. "*The* Thavo Domp?!"

The casino owner smiled broadly. "I see you've heard of me."

"*Heard of you?*" exclaimed Quell, tucking the chip into his waistcoat pocket. "I've spent *years* researching you! You're my idol—a self-made man I've spent my entire adult life trying to emulate. In fact, I just finished reading your autobiography for the sixth time last week. Your photo on the back cover does not do you justice."

Quell squinted at Thavo Domp's face. "You look a lot older than your publicity photographs."

Domp laughed. "They are rather out of date. I've been meaning to arrange a new photoshoot for some time."

"So... My winnings?" asked Quell. "When do I get the credits?"

"Whenever you want," promised Domp. "But surely

there's no hurry. Stay awhile, play a few more hands. You are, after all, one of our most accomplished customers."

Quell felt his chest swell with pride, but he forced the sensation down. "I don't know if I should..."

"Well, at least stay for a drink to celebrate your success," suggested Domp. "Nat," he began, turning to the croupier. "Please inform the bar staff that Mr. Quell's drinks are to be put on my personal account for the remainder of the evening."

"Really?" exclaimed Quell. "That's great! There are a few cocktails on the menu I've been wanting to try, but I just couldn't afford them."

"Well, now you can." The casino owner chuckled. "You *are* a millionaire, after all."

"But they're still free, right?" Quell queried. He looked at the croupier. "You heard him say that, didn't you?"

"Of course," Domp assured him. "Now, if you'd like to make your way back to the casino floor, I'll have Nat arrange for your winnings to be paid to you."

Excited, Lowlon Quell jumped to his feet and hurried to the padded red leather office door. As he opened it he heard the unmistakable chatter, bells and music of the various games. Smiling, he scampered down the stairs to rejoin the fun.

As the croupier started to follow him, Thavo Domp took her arm and pulled her toward him.

"Ply him with drink and make sure he doesn't leave without losing the majority of those million credits," he hissed. "Or I'll call in the debt your father owes to me."

Nat nodded, shaken. "Of course, sir."

5

Moon of Hann, Blue Diamond Casino, Gaming Floor

High Priest Jolio Phisk strode in through the main entrance of the casino, ignoring the shivering but smiling showgirls in tiny sequined bikinis and elaborate feather headdresses posing on either side of the lobby.

Inside, the sudden cacophony of slot machine jingles mixed with the sound of clattering coins caused him to wince. He always enjoyed his trips to the less moralistic of Taglen's twin moons, but it invariably took a short while to acclimate himself to the gaudy onslaught on the senses, especially after spending time in the pious atmosphere of the temple.

He passed row after row of slot machines, each topped with flashing lights and a video screen on which one tiered Z-list celebrity or another shouted why gamblers should choose the one and only credit-winning system they alone endorsed as a way of passing the time and spending their salaries.

Phisk shuddered at the sight of sleepy-eyed aliens from a dozen different worlds sitting on faux-leather stools, one hand or claw or tentacle clutching a large cup of coins while another appendage slid silver bits into the dazzling boxes of stolen dreams.

This place would be perfect if it weren't for the people.

At the bar, he gestured to a gum-chewing barmaid presumably hired more for the expanse of her chest than her ability to mix drinks. "Who's the duty manager tonight?"

"Zalah Gilt," drawled the woman, leaning forward so she could be heard over the deafening racket of a nearby arcade game tempting passers-by with a once-in-a-lifetime opportunity to win a speedboat.

The movement caused her gargantuan breasts to test the mettle of her official Blue Diamond corset. Thankfully —for Phisk, at least—the corset won this particular bout.

"Get him for me," he commanded.

"Sure, honey," said the barmaid. "You wanna drink while you're waitin'?"

Phisk shook his head and the barmaid shrugged and made for a phone receiver hanging next to the stockroom door at the back of the bar.

"Hey, come on, pal!" slurred a Taglenian sitting two stools away. He had half a dozen empty shot glasses scattered on the bar in front of him and he was rolling a pair of yellow multi-sided dice. "You should have a drink."

"No," said Jolio Phisk, flatly. "Thank you."

But the drinker would not be deterred. "Celebrate with me! I jus' won a million fucking credits, you know!"

Phisk regarded the man with a suspicious stare. "Congratulations."

"Well, it *was* a million. But I lost abou' fif-fifty thousand on a hand just now, so I'm takin' a break to clear my head. Come on, have a drink with me. I'm payin'."

Phisk didn't reply this time, but he didn't need to. A petite croupier with a pixie-like turned-up nose and a name tag which read Nat spotted the gambler and hurried over to escort him back to whichever gaming table was hers.

"There you are, Mr. Quell!" she exclaimed. "I've been looking everywhere for you. Come back and play with us. We're due to make a big payout, and I have a good feeling about you and your lucky dice."

Phisk watched as the man climbed down from his stool, stumbling slightly and having to be caught by the attractive croupier. "You're so nice to me." He grinned at the girl. "I think you're...you're jus' lovely."

" I think you're lovely, too," promised the croupier, snatching up the yellow dice from the bar and hooking her arm through Quell's. "Now, come on before someone else wins that next jackpot."

Amused by this miniature one-act play, Phisk watched as the uniformed girl steered her charge between the rows of slot-machines toward the slightly more sedate area of the casino floor where serious gamblers sat at any number of green-baize-covered tables.

"Your holiness!" cried a voice from behind him.

Jolio Phisk turned to find a slim man in a Blue Diamond blazer standing behind him. "Mr. Gilt," said the high priest, grasping the casino manager's hand and shaking it firmly. "Good to see you again."

"Excuse the delay," Zalah Gilt offered. "You didn't warn us you were coming, so I had to arrange your room at short notice."

He gestured for Phisk to lead on and the two men walked calmly toward the rear of the casino floor.

"I didn't know I was coming, myself," Phisk explained, "but we had a decent collection at the temple and I thought, 'On Persha's eyes, why not?'"

"Why not, indeed?" Gilt beamed.

They reached a line of four doors at the back of the vast room, each covered with the same deep-blue velvet as the walls to make them difficult to see from more than a few meters away.

Gilt removed a card with a silver chip embedded in the plastic but paused before using it in the lock beside the nearest door. "Now, I'm afraid Chastity is away on leave for a few days since her mom is unwell, but I've hired a new girl in her place and I think you're going to like her a lot. Very lithe; amazing flexibility."

Phisk scowled. "And the other?"

Zalah Gilt smiled. "Slutella is ready and waiting for you, and I made certain she has a pair of fingerless gloves and a fresh selection of unwashed vegetables per your requirements."

Jolio Phisk could barely contain his excitement as the casino manager turned to unlock the velvet-covered door.

Polarso Major, Faithiola Township

"Gilly Pradu!" announced Adina, reading the next name from the list on her clipboard. The young girl standing beside her gripped her free hand, eyes darting back and forth over the crowd of townspeople at the side of the field on which the ICS *Fortitude* had landed.

"Here!" cried an anxious female voice. "We're here!"

The crowd parted to allow a woman and man through to the front. They froze when they spotted Gilly with tears flowing down their cheeks.

"Mama! Papa!" yelled the child, releasing Adina's hand and racing barefoot across the recently-cut grass.

The mother dropped to her knees and spread her arms wide as Gilly approached. Soon the reunited family was lost in an embrace they had thought they would never share again.

The father looked at Jack and Tc'aarlat, who were standing to one side. "Thank you!" he said emotionally, his voice cracking. "Thank you so much."

"It's our pleasure," replied Jack, smiling.

He turned to Tc'aarlat as the family made their way to the dusty road beyond the field, still holding onto each other. "Makes you feel good, doesn't it? Getting kids back to their families like this."

The Yollin sneered. "It would, if it wasn't for Lord Golden Boy Von Fuck-trumpet over there."

Jack followed Tc'aarlat's gaze to where the rest of the rescued children were gathered around Draven. The blond pilot was making the group laugh by telling them jokes and performing sleight-of-hand tricks with blades of grass and a silk handkerchief he'd had tucked into his jacket pocket.

"Are you...jealous?" Jack inquired, trying his best to hide his grin.

"Of course not!" spat Tc'aarlat. "But, look at him! Taking all the glory. Where was he when we were banging heads trying to get the location of the slave market or busy finding new and interesting ways to fuck up those bollock-faced jizz-jockeys who think it's okay to buy and sell kids for fun and profit?"

Mist flew out the open doorway of the ship, soared over their heads, and landed lightly on Draven's shoulder, much to the delight of the gathering of children.

Tc'aarlat growled beneath his breath. "Fucking typical!"

"Ernil Morcab!" shouted Adina, looking at the group of children. A young boy around eleven years old flung his arms around Draven for a hug, then turned and ran to where Adina was waiting with an elderly lady.

"Granny!" he cried excitedly.

"That's enough!" barked Tc'aarlat. He stomped over to Adina and snatched the clipboard from her hands. "You take a break. I'll take over for a while."

"No, it's okay," said Adina. "I can carry on."

The Yollin fixed her with a hard stare. "I told you to take a break."

"O...K..." said Adina, her eyebrows raised. "If you insist."

"I do!" insisted Tc'aarlat. He glanced at the next two names on the list. "Laylo Kinna and Daw Restel." Two children broke away from the main group, looking warily at the crowd of locals as they tentatively made their way to the Yollin.

"Hurry up!" snapped Tc'aarlat. "We haven't got all day to hand you back to your loving parents!"

Shaking her head, Adina crossed to where Draven was now lying on the ground. The remaining half-dozen children had piled on top of him and were executing wrestling moves.

"I can't tell who's having the better time," she commented extending a hand to help him up. "You or the kids."

"Oh, it's definitely me." Draven smiled as he took her hand. He turned to the youngsters, who were waiting to see what he was going to do next to entertain them."

"OK," he said, fishing a copper coin from his pocket. "First one to catch Mist wins this pirate treasure!"

He twitched his shoulder to send Mist into the air, and with a happy *SKAWWW!* she flew toward the far end of the field with the giggling children on her tail.

"You're really good with them," said Adina. "Do you have children of your own?"

"Me? No, I haven't been so blessed," replied Draven, flipping the coin in the air, then tucking it back into his pocket. "How about you? Is there a Mr. Choudhury and lots of little Choudhurys running around somewhere?"

Adina shook her head. "No, just me," she admitted, keeping her eyes on the ground. "I have an uncle who lives in a care home but, other than him I have no family at all."

Draven's expression became more serious. "That's a real shame," he said softly. "I think family is important—as are friends. They can be like family, if you let them."

"Yeah, I guess so," agreed Adina, turning to look at her Yollin friend. Tc'aarlat was trying in vain to referee an argument between two mothers who each claimed one of the young females was *her* daughter.

Jack stood watching the proceedings with his arms folded and laughed as Tc'aarlat turned helplessly from one angry mother to the other.

"Jack and Tc'aarlat are good pals," said Adina. "I don't know where I'd be without them."

Draven pulled a pleading face. "Don't tell me you don't have room for a new friend to join in the fun."

Adina's cheeks beginning to redden again. "I wouldn't say that," she responded, finally meeting Draven's gaze.

Draven reached out to take Adina's hand and smiled. "You don't know how happy I am to hear that. And I promise that I'm a very good boy. I don't shed on the furniture or anything."

Adina looked confused. "You don't *what*?"

"Shed," repeated Draven. "My fur, I mean. You did realize I was a werewolf, didn't you?"

"What? Yes, of course." Adina laughed self-consciously and pulled her hand free of Draven's. She cast a glance at Jack, who was now involved in the row between the two furious women. "I'd better go. It looks as if the guys need some help over there."

"Yeah, sure." Draven pushed his hands into the pockets of his jeans. "I'll...er... I'll wait here for the kids to get back."

Adina nodded slightly and hurried to join the ongoing disagreement.

Draven watched her go, trying to work out what he'd said wrong.

If he hadn't been so lost in his thoughts, he might have noticed a pair of sharp brown eyes watching him from the shadows beyond the open doorway of the ship.

Moon of Persha, Maximum Security Prison, Conjugal Rights Trailer

Trace Byrn slumped back against the thin mattress of the bed, naked. Her hair was plastered to her forehead with sweat.

That had been incredible!

She turned to watch the heavily tattooed back of Vimor Malfic as it disappeared into the trailer's tiny bathroom, then looked up at the cracked paint on the ceiling as the thin wooden door slammed shut and water began to flow in the shower.

No one had ever made Trace feel like that before. Like she was being taken and consumed and enjoyed.

Their lovemaking had been passionate, animalistic, and raw—better than a hundred bubble baths at the same time.

She never wanted to feel any other way again.

Trace and Malfic had not exchanged more than a dozen words, most of them small talk, while the guard on duty had shown them to the door of the ancient trailer.

This was the venue made available to those inmates who had earned a period of privacy with their visitor. At first Trace had been a little self-conscious, knowing the guard remained right outside the door but once Malfic had begun to tear away her clothing all thought of propriety had been jettisoned.

Within minutes, the trailer had been rocking from side to side and she had been screaming at the top of her lungs. There was no way the guard could have any doubt what was happening inside.

She heard the shower stop running and took a deep breath, ready for a repeat performance. From what Malfic had told her in his letters, he had called in several favors to earn use of the conjugal rights trailer but their stay would be strictly limited.

They just had time to take a rocket ship to the stars once more.

The door opened and Malfic emerged. He was naked and wet, his hair tousled and skin glistening.

And, oh...the way he looked at her. Like she was the only thing he had ever wanted.

"You brought the computer chip?" he growled.

"Of course," Trace replied, lifting herself up on her elbows and patting a hand against her tummy. "I followed your instructions to the letter. But, I'll need to use the bathroom before you can get your hands on it."

Malfic's lips curled into a sneer beneath the thick black hair of his beard and mustache.

"I can't wait that long."

He lunged forward, hands reaching for her. Trace arched her back, pushing her forward, her nipples stiffening as she readied herself for round two.

But Malfic didn't touch her breasts. Instead he jabbed his fingertips hard against her stomach, his sharp fingernails digging into her soft, trembling flesh.

"Careful, honey!" she exclaimed. "I like it rough as much as the next girl, but that kinda hurts."

"Shut the fuck up!" spat Malfic, lifting one hand long enough to slap his newfound lover hard across the cheek.

Trace gasped as the shock of the blow sunk in. She brought up a hand to touch the stinging skin on her face, but that pain was quickly obscured by the searing agony farther down her body.

Malfic was using his fingers to tear her open.

Gripping handfuls of flesh, Vimor Malfic ripped open Trace Byrn's stomach. She screamed and fought to free herself from her attacker, the bed and trailer rocking as she struggled.

The guard outside would simply presume they were doing it again.

Blood sprayed from the tear in her flesh, coating the stained walls of the trailer with a fine red mist as Malfic dug deeper, working his fingers through the meat and gristle, pulling apart both organs and intestines as he rummaged around.

Trace felt her life force begin to seep away, the regret for the many opportunities and events she would never experience matching the physical pain of her disemboweling.

But worse than that was the shame. The knowledge that the beautiful things Vimor Malfic had said in his letters and poems were nothing more than a deception.

So many friends and family members had warned her not to stay in touch with "that criminal" or "that monster." They had told her no good would come of a relationship with a convicted murderer; that it would end badly and she was making the biggest mistake of her life.

It had been the *final* mistake of her life.

Finally, Malfic located her stomach and tore it open as if it were a bag of chips. Inside, awash with acid, were the remnants of the sandwich and juice she had bought and consumed on the shuttle flight from the planet this morning and, of course, the tiny computer chip this had all been about.

The only thing he had ever truly wanted from her.

After wiping the blood and gore from the chip, Malfic held it up to the single light bulb and smiled. On the bed, the bloodied body of Trace twitched as she tried to speak, to question his actions, to ask why.

Her lips moved slowly, but no sound came out.

She could no longer speak.

Instead, she cried.

Without looking down at her again Malfic returned to the bathroom, the computer chip clutched inside his bloodied fist.

The last thing Trace Byrn ever heard was the sound of water running as the shower started again.

6

ICS Fortitude, Crew Quarters

Adina cupped her hands under the faucet of the tiny sink in her cabin and splashed the ice-cold water on her face.

She plucked a threadbare towel from the end of her bunk and used it to pat herself dry, then inhaled deeply. The towel had been one of the few items she had been allowed to pack and take with her when she had left home to live with her Uncle Yousuf, and although after thousands of washes it no longer smelled of her parents' house, she still liked to imagine there was some lingering connection with the family she'd once had.

Carefully folding the towel and setting it aside, she opened the battered metal locker that served as both her closet and storage space and plucked a small bottle of pills from the top shelf.

Inside were dozens of tiny black tablets, each with a

single yellow dot stamped on one side. She took the medication to dampen certain strands of her DNA.

The strands that gave her the ability to transform into a wolf.

Adina had taken the medication—first purchased illegally from backstreet drug dealers by her uncle—ever since her first-ever transformation had ended disastrously.

Unaware that she carried the same lupine gene as her distant female ancestors, she had suddenly transformed on her thirteenth birthday in front of her entire family.

When she came to later, she was smeared with blood and the dead body of her mother was on the floor beside her.

Her father had disowned her at her mom's funeral, forcing her to move in with Uncle Yousuf.

He had tried hard to help Adina cope with her abilities, but the young girl had wanted no part of it. She'd even gone so far as to threaten suicide if her uncle couldn't find a way to stop her from ever transforming again.

She had been taking the DNA dampeners ever since but recently had cause to transform specific parts of her body into their wolf form in order to save lives during the Shadow's first mission.

She had even fully transformed when threatened by a terrified crowd of people attempting to flee from a gravity storm.

Jack and Tc'aarlat had both offered words of comfort and had tried to convince her that she shouldn't be ashamed of who she really was. But, it would take more than a few isolated incidents to undermine the belief that she had been responsible for her mother's death and the total destruction of her family.

So she continued to take the drug, which was now provided legally by pharmacists in the Federation thanks to her new benefactor, Nathan Lowell and his lovely wife.

She flipped the top off the pill bottle and shook out one of the tablets, then tossed it into her mouth and washed it down with some water from the sink.

As she tucked the medication bottle away there was a soft knock at the cabin door.

Adina closed the locker and checked her reflection in the mirror above the sink before opening the door.

Draven was standing outside.

"I think I owe you an apology," he told her immediately, "although I'll admit I have no idea what to apologize *for*."

"I don't know what you're talking about," Adina responded.

"Neither do I," admitted Draven. "I just know we were getting along really well and then a barrier came down. Did I say something wrong?"

"Of course not."

"Well, *something* happened," Draven insisted. "And whatever it was, I'm sorry for it."

Before Adina could comment, she and Draven were forced to grab the doorframe when the ship began to move.

"We're taking off," Adina told him. "And we're lucky Solo hasn't insisted that we—"

"This is Solo," the EI announced over the ship's comm. "Would all personnel please report to the bridge, where safety belts and harnesses are available to ensure the welfare of crew members and guests alike."

Adina smiled wryly. "And there it is."

"Look," Draven took Adina's hand, "I don't know what went wrong, but I'd like to fix it. Jack's offered to drop me off at the closest Federation base station. By way of an apology, would you do me the honor of having dinner with me when we get there?"

Adina pulled her hand free. "I... I don't know."

"Lunch, then," offered Draven with a sparkle in his eye. "Elevenses, a light snack, a breath mint..."

Despite her anxiousness Adina laughed. "A drink," she countered. "I'll let you buy me a drink."

"It's a deal." A beaming Draven held out his hand. Adina smiled as she shook it...and didn't pull away as quickly as the blond pilot had expected.

All of a sudden, the ship lurched hard to starboard and alarms shrieked through the speakers.

"Emergency! Emergency!" bellowed Solo. "A missile of unknown origin has locked onto the ICS *Fortitude*'s heat signature."

Adina pushed past Draven and ran for the bridge. "Not this shit again!"

Moon of Persha, Maximum Security Prison, Security Zone

Vimor Malfic tightened his grip on the terrified guard's arm and pushed him toward the entrance to the visitors' security area.

"Don't try anything stupid," he growled, jabbing the guard's own pistol into his ribs.

"N-no..." stammered the guard. "I won't."

Nerk Wassel had always enjoyed being the official assigned to watch over the prisoners who used the conjugal rights trailer.

While his colleagues moaned and complained when that particular duty was assigned to them, Wassel actually looked forward to it. The passion had well and truly evaporated from his marriage—if such a thing had ever really been there in the first place—and standing guard outside the rocking and juddering metal caravan while those inside grunted loudly and screamed in ecstasy was something of a turn-on.

In fact, there had been occasions when he'd been required to hastily fasten his trousers when the trailer door had opened unexpectedly.

As a result, he now enjoyed his duties farther around to the side of the courtyard in which the trailer was positioned. He'd heard of people who became excited at the prospect of being discovered mid-tug, but he knew it wouldn't be easy to find a new job if he was fired for indulging in a quick five-knuckle shuffle on the company's time.

He'd been very surprised when Vimor Malfic had requested use of the trailer during visiting hours and had been inclined to deny the request, like the majority of his fellow guards would have. That was until the guy in charge of checking the inmates' incoming mail had shown him the photos included in Malfic's sudden flurry of perfume-infused letters.

The floozy who was sending him the scantily-clad photographs—three of which he had snaffled for his own enjoyment before the letter was delivered to Malfic—was worth bending a few rules for.

Nerk Wassel had been pleasantly surprised when the woman had turned up for the visit. Usually these wannabe convict-fuckers sent prisoners pics from when they were much younger and more attractive, and frequently shots of other females entirely. By the time they showed up in person, the inmate in question was far too horny to complain about the deception. So long as there was a willing body to use and abuse, who cared if you had to close your eyes and imagine someone else?

Wassel swallowed hard when he saw the duty guards at the security station. His immediate boss Sergeant Tanx was in command.

If he somehow managed to get out of this fuck-up alive, Sergeant Tanx would almost certainly cut off the parts of his body he had been abusing when Malfic had burst of out the trailer and taken him by surprise.

Thankfully the criminal had allowed him to re-fasten his trousers before taking him hostage.

Briefly releasing his grip on Wassel's arm, Malfic stabbed the barrel of the gun into the guard's side a little harder, then produced some kind of silver chip—much like the one embedded in his own prison pass—and swiped it over the sensor on the door to the visitor lobby.

After the light on the lock turned green and the door unlocked with a *clunk*, Malfic took the guard's arm again. Then, raising his foot, he kicked open the door and dragged Wassel through it to the security zone with a furious snarl of rage.

"Every one of you donkey-fisters—get down on the ground now or this wank-happy shit-sucker gets a bullet through the heart!"

ICS *Fortitude*, Bridge

When Adina and Draven reached the bridge, Tc'aarlat was racing out.

"Tc'aarlat!" yelled Solo over the blaring alarms. "Get back in your seat and refasten your safety belt this minute!"

"Kiss my crusty Yollin ass!" he shouted as he dodged the two humans and continued running.

As Adina stepped onto the bridge, the ship swung sharply to port.

"There's another missile chasing us!"

Jack, clinging to the console in front of him, glanced over his shoulder. "And by all accounts, it's more powerful than the last one."

"Who's doing this?"

"Fuck knows!" replied Jack. "But whoever it is, they've taken quite a dislike to us. Solo, mute those *Gott Verdammt* alarms!"

Silence flooded the bridge.

"Or maybe they only dislike one of you," suggested Draven.

Adina's brow furrowed. "What do you mean?"

"Well, this could be an attack on the Shadows as a group, or perhaps one of you three have pissed off whoever's behind this to such an extent that they're willing to sacrifice innocent lives to get even."

"Well, I'm pretty sure I haven't annoyed anyone enough to warrant a price on my head," Jack told Draven as the ship suddenly dropped a few hundred meters. "Adina?"

"Not that I know of," Adina replied after she caught her balance. "Not unless my fifth-grade teacher Mrs. Swarbrick is still upset about the picture of her I drew on the girls' bathroom wall."

"That leaves you and Tc'aarlat," Jack pointed out.

"Can't be me," said Draven. "I wasn't on board when the first missile was launched, remember?"

"Speaking of Tc'aarlat, where was he heading?" asked Adina. "He shot out of here like a kid chasing an ice cream truck."

"No idea," replied Jack. "He just jumped up and—"

A new alarm began to sound and a small, red light began to flash on the main console.

"Shit, I *do* know where he is," spat Jack. "He's just activated the door to the *Pegasus'* hangar!"

By the time Adina and Draven reached the hangar Tc'aarlat was already sitting in the pilot's seat of the *Pegasus* II, impatiently running through the pre-flight checklist while the wide turntable it sat on spun the ship to face the rear doors.

Mist was motionless on his leather shoulderpad.

"Tc'aarlat!" yelled Adina breathlessly as she hammered on the tinted glass of the side window. "What the hell are you doing?"

The Yollin's voice responded tinnily via a speaker hidden somewhere beneath the craft's gleaming black paintwork. "What does it look like?" he demanded. "I'm gonna shoot down that bastard missile!"

"You can't!" countered Draven, peering in the window on the other side of the shuttle.

"Why not?" rumbled Tc'aarlat. "Because I'm not a super-cool hippie pilot like you?"

"No!" shouted Draven. "Because you'll be flying straight at the missile. I came at it from behind. The thing will most likely hit and destroy you before you can hit the switch to arm the forward guns!"

Tc'aarlat blinked a few times, obviously thinking this through. Then he shook his head and doubled down on his efforts to complete the checklist.

With a barely audible *click*, the turntable reached its destination and *Fortitude*'s rear doors began to open.

Adina and Draven looked at each other through *Pegasus'* windows.

"He won't listen!" exclaimed Adina. "If he goes out there, he'll end up killing himself and destroying the *Pegasus*. Then we'll have *no* way of stopping that fucking missile!"

Draven thought for a second, then turned his head and spoke aloud. "Solo, what type of main engines do you have?"

"Pulse-fusion-based ion drives, Draven," Solo replied. "Why?"

"Do they dump irradiated superheated plasma as a by-product after they've fired?"

"Yes, they do," Solo replied. "I use the plasma to power the ship's internal heating system."

The *Pegasus II* began to rise as the rear doors edged closer to fully open.

Adina glanced at the clear blue sky beyond them and saw the missile as it streaked toward them.

"Can you reroute that plasma and exhaust it through the waste ports connected to the main engines?" questioned Draven.

"Yes, of course," responded Solo. "But I don't see why I would ever—"

A metallic *CLUNK* rang out as the doors locked open and Tc'aarlat begin to pilot the *Pegasus II* toward the exit and the heat-seeking missile.

"*DO IT NOW!*" bellowed Draven.

Almost immediately a surge of gas burst from the ship's twin engines, flooding the air behind the *Fortitude* with a fine fog. The vapor partially blocked the incoming missile from view, but Adina could still hear its engine roaring as the deadly weapon flew closer.

As quickly as the mist had appeared it evaporated, to be replaced by trails of pale-blue goop. They spat from the engine vents in viscous trails that converged on the missile as it shot toward them.

"*DOWN!*" cried Draven.

He and Adina threw themselves to the floor behind the *Pegasus II* just as the heat-seeking missile exploded. A blast of red-hot air filled the hangar, peeling the paint from the body of the shuttle and singeing the fine hairs coating Adina's arms.

Everything fell silent.

ICS Fortitude, Rear Cargo Bay

"How the fuck does he do it?" spat Tc'aarlat, stomping up and down the empty cargo bay. Mist watched her master with interest from a metal beam high above.

Jack glanced at Draven, who was applying burn salve from the first aid kit to the singed skin of Adina's arms and face. He took care to ensure there was enough cream left for himself. "Do what?"

"Stop a sodding heat-seeking missile with no more than an idea and come out of it with a motherfucking tan?!"

Jack frowned. "I wouldn't call it a tan exactly. He and Adina were burned by the blast of scorched air that blasted into the hangar after the explosion."

Tc'aarlat's eyes were bulging. "Does he look burned to *you*?"

Jack looked back at the Etheric Federation pilot. "No, not really." He chuckled. "He may be sore for a few days, but it does look good on him."

He raised a finger to stop the Yollin before he could continue his rant. "But they were both very fortunate not to have been badly hurt. Look at what the blast did to the paintwork on the front of the new *Pegasus*."

"That's another thing!" moaned Tc'aarlat, eliciting an exasperated sigh from Jack. "Nathan's going to do his nut when he finds out we've totaled another multi-million-credit space cruiser."

Jack pulled out his tablet and swiped through the photographs of the damage to the *Pegasus II* Solo had taken to send back to the *Meredith Reynolds*. In addition to the scorched paint, the metal framework at the front of the craft had buckled from the extreme pressure of the blast and the toughened glass of the windows displayed radiating burn marks.

"It's hardly totaled," he countered. "The damage is superficial at best. Plus, the thing was strong enough to save you from being hurt."

"*Pffft!*" spat Tc'aarlat.

Jack raised his eyebrows. "*Pffft?*" he questioned. "What's '*Pffft?*'"

"I'd have been fine," the Yollin asserted. "Exoskeleton, remember?"

"Is that why you've been chugging painkillers like candy for the nasty headache you got when you fainted earlier?"

"Yollin skulls are delicate!" Tc'aarlat protested, reaching up to prod the back of his head tenderly. "And I didn't *faint*."

"Yes, you did," countered Adina as she and Draven joined them. "I was there."

"You two have finished oiling each other up then?" Tc'aarlat scoffed.

"Don't be like that!" warned Adina. "We'd have all been floating around in tiny pieces if it hadn't been for Draven."

"That's true," agreed Jack, reaching over to shake the pilot's hand. "We're all very grateful for your quick thinking."

"*Pffft!*"

Jack glared at his Yollin counterpart. "We're *all* grateful."

"Suppose so..." muttered Tc'aarlat glumly, reluctantly taking Draven's outstretched hand. "But I still say—"

"Excuse me, Captain Marber," interrupted Solo. "You have an incoming video communication from Nathan Lowell."

"Oh, shit!" Tc'aarlat grunted. "He's heard about the *Pegasus* already!"

"Don't be ridiculous," Jack said, turning to face the EI's avatar on a nearby wall screen. "Tell Nathan we're on our way."

Moon of Hann, Red Light District, Back Alley

The stolen police shuttle landed in a deserted alley deep within the red-light district, its telescopic legs digging holes in the poorly-maintained tarmac.

The pilot's-side door opened with a *hisss* and Vimor Malfic climbed out, stretching his arms wide. He took a deep lungful of air and grinned somewhere beneath his thick black beard.

"Can't you just taste the depravity?"

"All I can taste is whatever had soaked into that filthy

rag you stuffed into my mouth at the prison parking lot!" complained Nerk Wassel.

Malfic stooped to peer inside the shuttle. The guard he had taken hostage during his escape was sitting uncomfortably in the copilot's seat, his wrists and ankles bound with strong plastic zip-ties.

The felon flipped the catch on the ship's glove box and rooted around inside until he found a knife, presumably confiscated from some prior passenger.

Wassel stiffened as the blade swished across the front of his body, cutting the restraint binding his hands together. He then repeated the action with the guard's feet.

After spinning the knife in his fingers, Malfic straightened and slipped it into the waistband of his sweatpants.

With permission to use the prison's conjugal rights trailer, Vimor Malfic had also been allowed to change out of his prison-duty orange jumpsuit into something more comfortable—and less ardor-dampening.

"So, is that it now?" the kidnapped guard asked as he rubbed the red marks on his wrists. "Am I free to go?"

"What do *you* think?" growled Malfic, delving into the glove box again and producing a radio scanner. He flicked the power switch and, after a sharp burst of static, confirmed that he was able to listen in on communications between police headquarters and patrol officers.

He switched the radio off to conserve the battery and gestured for Wassel to get out of the ship. "Let's go, little piggy!"

Wassel sighed and opened the door on his side of the ship. "Yes, sir," he muttered as he clambered into the night air and looked around to try to get his bearings.

He'd only been to the Moon of Hann once before, on a long weekend with some of his fellow recruits while they were at the police academy on Taglen.

The six law enforcement rookies had saved their meagre trainee-level pay for several weeks while they waited for their time off to align so they could jump on the free public transport offered by one of the large casinos.

They'd begun the weekend confidently, accepting complimentary drinks from and flirting with the attractive waitresses on the short spaceflight to the moon.

Once on Hann they had quickly immersed themselves in the decadent ambience, following every gaudy ad tempting them to drink deep, party hard, and win big.

Everyone was out of cash a little over an hour later.

The remainder of the weekend had been spent in the single dreary hotel room they had booked for all of them, believing it would only be used as a base to freshen up, change clothes, and exchange high-fives as they passed each other en route from one exciting conquest to the next.

The room had then been a temporary home to the six hungry and nervous young men, who survived on a diet of free crackers and ketchup packets while hiding from the pimps who managed the girls they'd leered at on the street corners.

The lowest point of the weekend had come when the police recruits had been arrested for scavenging through dumpsters behind a twenty-four-hour Shrillexian restaurant and shipped back to the academy in a police transport vehicle.

One swift dismissal later, Wassel had found himself on

the fast-track to life as a low-paid guard at the prison on the Moon of Persha.

His first visit to Persha's sister moon was something he had worked hard to forget.

This second visit wasn't shaping up to be much of an improvement.

Malfic gestured for Wassel to follow and strode confidently down the alley, making no attempt to stick to the shadows. The escapee even began whistling. It was as if he were daring the authorities to find and arrest him.

When they reached the end of the alley, the two men stepped into the street and were immediately assaulted by the sights, sounds, and smells that pervaded the Moon of Hann.

Everywhere they looked there were flashing neon signs advertising everything from gambling dens to strip-clubs, and much more.

Bass-heavy music pounded from inside just about every building, almost—but not quite—drowning out the shouts of rowdy revelers and the screams of those enjoying worse fortune.

The moon's artificially-heated air was thick with competing aromas: fast food, cheap perfume, and even cheaper alcohol.

The Moon of Hann was a debauched cesspit of deviance, lust, and greed.

Vimor Malfic felt right at home.

"Move it," he growled, pushing a path through the throng of alien carousers swarming the sidewalk.

Wassel briefly considered allowing himself to be swept along by the tide of thrill-seekers, getting lost in the crowds, and finding somewhere to call the authorities and hide out until he could be rescued.

But every time he prepared himself to dart into some dark doorway, almost all manned by some kind of scowling lifeform that looked like a cross between a killer shark and an angry mountain, Malfic would glower at him to ensure his hostage kept up.

So he did.

Both sides of the street were lined with brightly lit windows, behind which gyrated men, women, things with tentacles, and in one instance what appeared to be a dense cloud of vapor in a pink leather bikini.

There was even one block populated entirely by raunchily rotating robots, causing Wassel to picture an assembly line of exhausted and bored engineers putting these degenerate droids together while computer techs in an adjoining room coded stilted conversations crammed with come-ons and assorted erotic moans and groans.

Each goldfish bowl-like cubicle sported a bed, a rack of costumes, and an array of bizarre toys and props designed to boggle the mind and titillate every other part of the body.

Yet, despite their suggestive expressions and lewd gestures, the cavorters showed little to no enthusiasm for the various depravities offered behind the thick panes of glass.

Gangs of sightseers crowded outside these windows giggling and drooling at the provocative displays put on by the sex-workers within, each gesturing for the tempted tourists to step on up and take a swift yet expensive trip to the heavens and back.

Every now and again one of the randy revelers would nod to the feisty figure behind the window. At that point an equally transparent door would open to allow them inside with their fists full of cash and the rest of their bodies overflowing with pent-up lust.

The alien on offer would slide a faded red curtain across the proceedings, and the gathering outside would move as one to another of the gaudily-lit displays of flesh and fulfillment.

Despite the ongoing hostage situation, Wassel found himself enjoying the chance to ogle these purveyors of pleasure as he trailed along behind Malfic. He wasn't sure where his captor was headed, but he began to wish his need to get there was less urgent so that he might have more time to peruse the delights on offer.

He was so engrossed in one window—behind which a Jagwa and a Skaine were wrestling in an inflatable pool filled with gravy—that he failed to notice Malfic had stopped and walked into him hard.

"Oof!"

Malfic sneered down at the distracted guard before rapping his knuckles on a narrow wooden door wedged between two of the glass cubicles.

After a brief moment a shrill whiny voice called out from the other side, "What's the password?"

"Open this fucking door right now or I'll ram it right up your rusty sheriff's badge!" spat Malfic.

There was a hurried sliding back of bolts and unfastening of locks, then the door creaked open a few inches and a pair of dull and partially crossed eyes peered out of the shadows within.

"Well, you took your damn time!"

ICS *Fortitude*, Bridge

The *Fortitude*'s three permanent crew members settled into their seats in front of the main viewscreen and Draven folded down a temporary seat fixed to the rear wall.

"Thank you for joining me, Shadows," began Nathan once everyone was settled, "and Draven, of course. There's something very important I need to discuss with you."

"The new *Pegasus* is fine!" Tc'aarlat blurted.

Nathan blinked and was silent for a few seconds. "I'm glad to hear it," he said, his brows furrowing. "Let's hope this model manages to stay in one piece for more than one mission."

The Yollin's eyes went wide and he began to laugh a little too loudly. "Bwa-ha-ha-ha-ha! Good one, Nathan! Very funny!"

Nathan looked quizzically toward Jack. "Is everything okay, Captain?"

After throwing Tc'aarlat an angry glance Jack nodded. "He fell and hit his head earlier," he explained. "Please continue..."

"We've gotten reports of a break-out from a maximum-security prison on one of the moons of Taglen," said Nathan, tapping the screen of his tablet. "The escaped prisoner, Vimor Malfic, is an extremely nasty piece of work."

The viewscreen split vertically with Nathan's video feed on one half and a mugshot of the heavily bearded and sneering Malfic on the other.

"*Gott Verdammt!*" cursed Adina. "He queued up twice when they were handing out the ugly, didn't he?"

"Malfic is incredibly dangerous," continued Nathan. "He murdered at least one individual during his escape, and he won't have any compunction against killing again."

"Do you know where this guy is now?" asked Draven.

"Not exactly," Nathan replied. "According to our latest intel, he stole a police shuttle from outside the prison and blasted off as his guards gave chase. The ship he took is not a long-range craft, so it's likely he's still somewhere in the local system."

"How can we help?" queried Jack.

"You're not too far from a gate which will take you to within an hour's flight of Taglen and its twin moons," Nathan's fingers danced on the screen of his tablet again. "I'm sending over everything we have on the world and on Malfic. Get there and see if there's anything you can do to assist the local authorities."

"Will do," agreed Jack, pulling out his tablet as it dinged to acknowledge the arrival of Nathan's files. "We'll keep you updated."

"Good luck," Nathan offered and the video feed ended.

"Well, it looks like you'll be with us a little while longer," Jack said, spinning his chair to face Draven.

"Are you sure?" Tc'aarlat asked. "I mean, there's nothing to keep him from going back to his official duties, what-ever they are, if we can drop him off somewhere on the way to this gate."

"Hey, I don't mind staying a while," Draven relayed with a grin. He gave a wink in Adina's direction. "I like hanging out with you guys, and who knows...I might even be able to help you with this mission."

"Always good to have another pair of hands," Adina remarked.

"It depends what you plan to do with them," murmured Tc'aarlat as he turned back to his section of the bridge's control console.

Jack set his tablet aside and looked at the face on the main viewscreen. "Solo, plot a course for the gate Nathan recommmended."

"Of course, Captain," the EI responded. "Just as soon as all personnel have fastened their safety belts and harnesses."

Draven opened his mouth to comment, but Adina spoke before he could. "Just do what she asks. You'll never hear the end of it otherwise."

Shrugging, Draven buckled in while the rest of the crew attended to their harnesses.

Safely secured, they waited for Solo to display the map of their calculated route and fire up the engines.

But nothing happened.

"Is there a problem, Solo?" Jack asked.

"Not at all, Captain," Solo replied. "I'm just waiting for everyone to secure their safety equipment before embarking."

Jack glanced around the cramped bridge, checking that everyone had properly fastened their belts. "All four of us are strapped in, Solo."

"That is correct, Captain. However, the young girl hiding in the level-three food storage unit is not."

8

ICS Fortitude, Level Three, Rear Storage Unit

The four crew members approached the open doorway to the storage unit as quietly as they could. The lights were off inside and, beyond the vague mountain-range shape of towering stacks of non-perishable food, nothing was visible.

Tc'aarlat pressed a hand to Draven's chest, his mandibles crossing.

"I'll handle this," he mouthed.

Draven smiled and shrugged. Satisfied, the Yollin nodded at Jack and Adina confidently and took a step toward the open door.

"You in there...stowaway" he began sternly. "Come out slowly with your hands in the air and no one needs to get hurt!"

As he finished speaking, a large can of chopped tomatoes came sailing out of the darkness and struck Tc'aarlat in the right eye.

81

The Yollin staggered backward with his hands clamped to his face. "Shitting ass-bastard sacks of crap!" he thundered, stomping back and forth.

Adina darted to his aid as Jack and Draven shared a look of concern and took up positions on either side of the storage unit's entrance.

"My name is Captain Jack Marber," Jack called out. "It's OK, you're not in any trouble—"

"Yes, she fucking is!" growled Tc'aarlat.

"You're not," Jack insisted. "We just want to talk to you, that's all."

There was a sudden *thud* from inside the unit, causing Tc'aarlat to take an involuntary step back.

But no reply.

"Hello?" called Draven. "Are you by yourself in there? Besides all the boxes of food, I mean."

Silence.

Adina took a deep breath and stepped up to the doorway, in clear view of whoever was hiding inside.

"What's your name?" she asked, calmly. "I'm Adina. Adina Choudhury."

For a moment, nothing, then...

"Callis."

The voice was young, female, and scared.

Adina smiled.

"Hi, Callis," she replied. "That was a pretty good shot with the tomatoes just now."

"What the fu—" Adina's glare cut off Tc'aarlat's protest.

"I can tell you're able to take care of yourself," she continued. "And that's good. It really is."

Silence again.

Adina flicked an uncertain glance in Jack's direction. He nodded, urging her to continue.

She took a deep breath.

"I can't imagine what those slave traders must have done to you," Adina offered. "But it was wrong. Very wrong. That's why we came to help you and your friends."

"They weren't my friends," replied the girl. "They were just a bunch of little kids."

Draven gave Adina a thumbs-up. Tc'aarlat continued to pace behind her, wincing each time he blinked.

"I saw that, Callis," Adina agreed. "They were all scared. I bet they were glad they had you around to protect them."

Back to silence.

"I certainly would have been."

A beat, then...

"I should have killed them. I was *going* to kill them."

Adina spotted movement in the shadows of the unlit room and took another step forward.

"I'm sorry if we spoiled that for you," she said. "It would have been useful to have you on our team."

Back to silence.

"You must be hungry," remarked Adina. "Are you?"

"There's a big piece of chocolate cake in the galley," she added. "Jack won it in the gun battle when we found you, but I'm sure he'd be happy to share it if you'd like some."

A thin dark-skinned teenage girl with matted black hair and red-ringed eyes appeared in the doorway of the storage room. She wore a stained hand-stitched singlet and mismatched scuffed shoes.

Jack and Draven held their respective breaths. Tc'aarlat stopped pacing and turned to look at her.

Adina smiled and reached toward the teen. "It's going to be okay."

Moon of Hann, Red Light District

Mildew Fester leaned heavily on a battered old walking cane as he led Vimor Malfic and Nerk Wassel up the narrow staircase toward the second-floor apartment door.

He pulled a jangling bunch of keys from a clip on his belt and opened the door's six separate locks, then silently gestured for the two men to follow as he stepped inside.

The interior of the apartment was a stark contrast to the bright lights and neon glitz of the street below. Low-wattage bulbs did their best to pierce the dreary gloom, but they were fighting a losing battle.

Paisley-patterned paper peeled from the walls, the edges dangling over a torn lounge suite whose faded brown upholstery clashed with a carpet which may possibly have featured a green and orange pattern in some former life. Now it was difficult to tell where the stains ended and design began.

Fester slumped into a battered armchair, sending up a mushroom cloud of dust. He reached for a near-empty bottle of some undefined gray liquor and poured a shot into a grubby coffee cup.

"You wanna drink?" he wheezed, cradling the cup in his ink-stained fingers.

Vimor Malfic shook his head, not bothering to extend the invitation to his hostage.

Wassel perched on the edge of the couch, his eyes flicking from one towering pile of aging papers to the next. Between these stacks sat crumpled grocery-store boxes overflowing with electrical gadgets, tangled power cords, and an assortment of outdated computer components.

Vimor remained standing, waiting patiently until their host had finished slurping at his drink. "You get what I asked for?"

Fester nodded, wincing as the alcohol burned his throat. "Most of it," he wheezed, setting the cup down and pouring the last dregs from the bottle.

After shaking it to ensure every last drop of the grim liquid escaped its container he lowered the bottle to the floor beside his chair, where it clattered against a collection of similarly drained brothers and sisters.

"I take it your little friend got the chip I made past security," Mildew commented, gazing up at Malfic. The villain's vast frame seemed to fill any empty space in the room, his thick, dark curled hair brushing the peeling paint of the ceiling.

"She sure did." Malfic laughed darkly. "I had a real fun time extracting that from her."

Mildew Fester made an attempt to join the felon's amusement by smiling, although it was like no smile Nerk Wassel had ever witnessed.

The few teeth Fester still retained ownership of were the color of dark mustard, interspersed with two which were so rotten and black they only became visible when they rattled against the off-white ceramic of his coffee cup.

"What about him?" Fester asked with a frown.

Vimor Malfic turned to glare down at Wassel as though

he had only just remembered the guard was there. "I needed collateral," he growled. "Once I've got everything I'll slit his throat."

Wassel's eyes grew wide in alarm. "What, don't I get a say in this?"

Malfic growled deep in the back of his throat. "Shut it!"

His impending fate sinking in, Wassel watched as Mildew Fester climbed unsteadily to his feet using his cane for support. The old man opened the door of an ancient wardrobe and took a thick envelope from the top shelf.

"Local currency, identity papers, and immigration visas for any of the five planets of the Ordanian Hub," he said, handing over the package.

Malfic slid out the forged ID card and read the name stamped on the surface. "Crispin Cottingly?" he queried. "Do I look like a fucking 'Crispin' to you?"

Fester shrugged and turned back to the wardrobe. "There were only two tourist deaths on Hann in the past week," he explained. "It was either that or Dorothy Spunge."

Sneering, Malfic tucked the paperwork away and took a cracked leather gym bag and a wash kit from his decrepit colleague.

"Bathroom's that way." Fester jerked his thumb over his shoulder.

Vimor Malfic fired a threatening stare in Wassel's direction and made for a door in the far wall. "Stay!"

"Hey, I'm not some kind of pet!" countered Wassel as Malfic left the room, keeping his voice low enough to ensure he wasn't heard.

Once the bathroom door closed he spun to face Mildew

Fester. "Look, I'm just a lowly prison guard. No one important. Malfic's free now; I'll only hold him up. What say you just let me slip out when your back's turned, huh? I'll make it worth your while..."

Fester appeared to consider the guard's offer for a moment, then he reached down the side of the cushion on his chair and produced a scuffed pistol, which he aimed at Wassel's chest. Hand trembling, the old man raised his thumb and pulled back the hammer.

"He told you to stay."

Half an hour later Malfic emerged from the bathroom looking like a different person.

He had shaved his beard, revealing a strong, square jaw studded with ancient scars. And the shearing hadn't stopped there. The felon had shaved his head completely bald.

The effect was as horrifying as it was dramatic. Nerk Wassel wouldn't have imagined his kidnapper could look any scarier, but this was a whole new level of terror.

It looked as though someone had taken a razor to a four-hundred-pound gorilla.

The resemblance wasn't helped by the cheap nylon business suit Malfic had barely managed to squeeze himself into. The silver material bulged, threatening to launch the two brave buttons that had undertaken the thankless task of keeping the jacket closed at some unsuspecting citizen.

The shirt collar had no hope of completely circling the escapee's tree-trunk-thick neck, so he had left it open and loosely knotted a bright red tie sporting pictures of what appeared to be penguins—but could just as easily be tiny nuns—like some kind of slender scarf.

Clearly whatever shoes Fester had procured had been too small for his client's immense feet, because he still wore his prison-issue slip-on sneakers.

"Did you find the guns?" asked Fester.

Malfic snatched up the gym bag and pulled out two sleek black weapons, both much more modern and sophisticated than the revolver Mildew Fester was now tucking back down the side of his seat.

When he pressed the pad of his index finger against the trigger of one of the blasters, a slender beam of laser light shot out from the gun's optical sight. Malfic aimed the glowing red dot at the middle of Wassel's now sweat-coated forehead, his upper lip curled into a shit-eating grin.

"Each one fires an ionized torus of super-heated plasma at its intended target," explained Fester, rummaging among his collection of liquor bottles for one with a few remaining drops nestled at the bottom. "You can set 'em to auto-repeat short bursts or simply produce a solid stream, depending on the composition and design of your target's armor."

Satisfied, Malfic released the trigger and switched off the laser guide. Nerk Wassel began to breathe again.

He tucked the pair of guns into the gym bag. "What about a ship?" he rumbled. "The piss-poor police shuttle I stole can't travel through interplanetary space. I need something bigger and more powerful."

"That's the only area where I was forced to compromise," responded Fester. "My usual guy was picked up last weekend for dealing in stolen warp drives and all his vehicles were impounded."

"So, what now?"

"I know another guy," said Fester, plunging a hand into his trouser pocket and pulling out a creased business card. He handed it over. "Zalah Gilt. He's a gaming floor manager at the Blue Diamond Casino over on Victory Boulevard. His ships are more expensive, but they're fast and virtually untraceable."

Malfic scowled. "*Virtually* untraceable?"

"He has his crew steal them from habitual gamblers." Mildew Fester shrugged. "Tells 'em they lost their pride and joy on the turn of a card while blasted on hard liquor. Those who doubt him are usually too embarrassed to go to the authorities, but there's always the exception to the rule."

Vimor Malfic grunted his understanding. Swinging the gym bag over his shoulder, he turned for the stairs leading down to the street.

"What about him?"

Malfic turned back to find Fester scowling at Nerk Wassel.

"You're not leaving him here."

"OK," Malfic snarled, then sighed. "But I can't have him trailing round after me dressed like that."

Wassel looked down at his gray guard uniform, then back up as Fester pushed himself out of the armchair and opened the wardrobe again. The old man ran his gnarled fingers along a row of hangers holding an entire rainbow's worth of brightly-colored outfits.

"Anything from the second rail and be quick about it."

Moon of Hann, Blue Diamond Casino, Gaming Floor

Lowlon Quell threw his head back and tossed another complimentary shot of Torcellan vodka down his throat.

The croupier ran a fresh deck of cards through her automatic shuffler and slotted them into the dealer's shoe, keeping one eye on her now-inebriated customer and the other on the location of the nearest waiter.

As instructed, she was keeping the supply of free drinks flowing, gradually wearing down Quell's ability to concentrate and ensuring he lost another chunk of his earlier winnings with each successive hand.

"Dealing," announced Nat as she slid cards for the table's three players from the mouth of the shoe. "Place your bets."

Lowlon Quell raised a hand and tried his best to focus on her. "Not f'me thisss time, Natty," he slurred, the heel of his boot clanging against the table's footrest as he made an attempt to climb down from his stool. "I need t'going home."

Nat glanced nervously at the window in the casino owner's office, doing her best not to react when her suspicion that she was being watched was confirmed. "Come on, Lowlon!" she cooed seductively. "The night is young. There's still time to win even *more*..."

She handed over Quell's final card and gently stroked her fingertips over the back of his hand, ignoring the sudden knot of guilt building inside her chest.

"And I get off work in a couple of hours, you know."

Lowlon Quell blinked hard, flashing an innocent smile

to all three of the croupier's faces as they swam about in his field of vision. Pausing to blow the conflicted croupier a kiss, he slid a stack of yellow chips across the soft surface of the table.

"Ten thousssand on making twenty-eight exxxactly!"

9

ICS Fortitude, Galley

Jack stood near the sink watching Adina and the teen stowaway Callis devour what remained of the crew's chocolate cake.

Adina wasn't able to get more than a few mouthfuls before the dessert was gone.

Tc'aarlat pressed an icepack against his throbbing eye and grunted. "For someone who's been living in one of our food storage units she can sure put it away."

"Nearly all of that unit is canned food," Jack reminded him. "Unless she has a stealth can-opener secreted somewhere, I doubt she's been able to eat very much at all."

"Well, she's making up for it now."

"Could you grab the slices of bistok shoulder from the cooler?" Adina called.

"Sure," Jack said, reaching for the refrigerator door. "We've still got some of that bird with the unpronounceable name we picked up on Alma Nine as well. The one that tastes like fried chicken. Want that, too?"

Adina looked at Callis, eyebrows raised.

"Yes, please," replied the teenager through a mouthful of cake.

Mandibles twitching, Tc'aarlat joined Jack as he searched the shelves of the refrigerator. "We'll have to find somewhere to drop her off before she eats us out of ship and home!"

Jack grabbed two platters of meat and closed the cooler door with his elbow. "She's hungry!" he responded. "You would be too if you'd just spent the past however-many years living on slave rations."

"Doesn't mean it's our job to feed her up again!" the Yollin grumbled.

Jack slid the platters onto the table and sat in one of the free chairs. "How old are you, Callis?"

The girl stopped chewing for a second, her eyes flicking from Jack to Adina.

"It's OK," said Adina gently, reaching out to take Callis' hand. "Jack's our captain. He'll do everything he can to protect you."

Jack nodded. "We all will," he promised, looking to where Tc'aarlat was standing. "Won't we?"

The Yollin sighed, lifted the icepack from his eye, and gently probed at the bruised area with his fingertips. "Yes, of course."

"I'm seventeen," replied Callis softly. "At least I think I am. It was hard to keep track of the time while I was..." Her voice trailed away.

"How long were you with the slavers?" Adina asked.

"They took me when I was six," Callis replied. She set down her fork, eyes gazing into some unknown distance. "And not just me. They took all the children from my village."

"We returned those children to their homes again," Tc'aarlat pointed out. "Or at least everyone we could find. Any idea why your family wasn't there to collect you?"

Callis didn't speak for a moment.

"They were," she replied quietly.

Jack exchanged a concerned glance with Adina and Tc'aarlat. "Your parents were waiting at the meeting point? You saw them?"

The teen nodded, silent.

Adina took the teenager's hand again and squeezed. "Then why didn't you go with them? Why didn't you go home?"

Callis' eyes grew wet with tears. "When the slavers came they raided our houses, looking for children and attacking anyone who stood in their way. Many parents were badly injured or even killed as they tried desperately to protect their young ones. But not my parents..."

"They didn't try to stop you from being taken?" asked Adina.

"No," hissed Callis with a small shake of her head. "They offered me to those bastards. They sold me to them!"

Jack sat back in his chair. "I'm sorry."

"Please don't take me back there," Callis pleaded. "I don't ever want to see them again. I'd rather be back with the slavers than that."

"We won't," Jack promised. "We'll find somewhere safe for you."

"Easy to say," Tc'aarlat commented, "but where? We've still got to drop His Royal Gorgeousness off. Speaking of which, where is he?"

"Up on the bridge," said Jack. "He's been going through the files Nathan sent for this mission."

Tc'aarlat's mandibles tapped together angrily. "What? That's need-to-know information for the Shadows' eyes only! Loose nips sink ships, Jack!"

With that he stomped out of the galley.

Sighing, Jack jumped to his feet. "I'd better..."

"It's okay." Adina smiled. "I'll stay here with Callis."

The captain nodded and hurried after Tc'aarlat. "It's loose *lips*, you bozo!"

Moon of Hann, Red Light District

Nerk Wassel scurried beside Vimor Malfic, keeping his eyes fixed on the pavement and trying hard to ignore the wolf-whistles and catcalls of passers-by.

"Hey, sweetie! Your place or mine?"

"Woohoo! Get a load of that guy over there!"

"Yeah, work it, baby!"

The lime-green rubber jumpsuit was the only outfit in Mildew Fester's wardrobe that had come anywhere close to fitting him.

Worse, now that Malfic had shaved his beard, Wassel could clearly see his captor's satisfied sneer as the suit squeaked and farted with each of his hurried steps.

The guard tugged on Malfic's sleeve. "Can you at least slow down a little?" he demanded. "I get that you're in a hurry, but this isn't exactly the easiest gear to move in."

For the past two blocks Wassel had been attempting to walk with his legs as wide apart as possible. This had the desired result of reducing the embarrassing noises emanating from the suit, but made it look as though he had recently soiled himself.

Malfic's response was little more than a snarl and he pointed to a bright animated sign halfway along the next block displaying a shimmering blue gemstone.

They had arrived at the Blue Diamond Casino.

ICS *Fortitude*, Bridge

Tc'aarlat stormed onto the bridge and made straight for the navigator's seat, where Draven was reading a page of text on a tablet.

"Give me that!" barked the Yollin, snatching it from Draven's hands and hurling it to the ground. The gadget shattered into pieces.

"What did you do that for?" demanded Draven, jumping to his feet.

"You shouldn't be reading that stuff!" yelled Tc'aarlat. "That is top-secret information for official members of this team!"

Draven scowled. "My emails are top secret?"

Tc'aarlat's mandibles quivered. "Your emails?"

"Yep," nodded Draven. "I thought I'd check my inbox while you lot were busy with that kid."

Tc'aarlat blinked.

"Oh, and I hope you don't mind," continued Draven, "but I couldn't get my tablet to connect to the ship's network for some strange reason—so I borrowed yours."

Teeth clamped tightly closed, Tc'aarlat looked down at the broken glass, cracked plastic, and smashed circuit boards that had made up the device. "No, that's fine," he croaked. "Help yourself."

"I see you two are getting along better now," Jack remarked as he strode through the doorway, sat in the pilot's seat, and spun to face his console. "Solo, can you give us the lowdown on the info Nathan sent over regarding the planet Taglen and its twin moons, please?"

"Of course, Captain," the EI responded. "One second while I compile the relevant intelligence."

Jack glanced down at the shattered tablet as Tc'aarlat slowly took his own chair. "You'll want to get that cleaned up before someone steps on it and hurts themselves."

Tc'aarlat nodded. "I'll get to it in a moment."

He leaned toward Jack, jerking a thumb over his shoulder. "Do you think we should be reviewing this stuff with you-know-who here?"

Jack glanced at Draven, receiving a friendly smile in return. "Hmmm... You're right," he replied, thoughtfully. "This is delicate info and should be for official members of the Shadows only."

"Exactly!" hissed Tc'aarlat. The Yollin reached into a small bowl of the treats he shared with Mist and popped one into his mouth.

"Leave it to me," said Jack. He spun in his chair again, this time to face the navigation desk. "Draven, how would you feel about becoming part of the team until we've got this prison break thing under control? You'd become an official member of the Shadows."

Tc'aarlat almost choked. "*WHAT?*"

"I'd love to, Jack, thank you," Draven replied. "As long as that's all right with Adina and Tc'aarlat, of course."

"I'm sure Adina won't have a problem with it at all," insisted Jack. "Tc'aarlat?"

The Yollin's mandibles were quivering. "No, that's perfectly fine," he said as calmly as he could. "You know me, Jack—the more, the murderer!"

Jack frowned. "I think you mean, 'the more, the *merrier.*'"

Tc'aarlat spun back to face the viewscreens. "I know what I mean," he muttered under his breath.

Solo's face appeared on the screens. "I have that data for you now, Captain."

Jack and Draven grabbed their tablets to take notes. Tc'aarlat sighed and folded his arms.

"The planet of Taglen," Solo explained, "suffered centuries of civil war, with opposing political parties raising armies in an effort to eradicate their enemies and seize control."

"Sounds like a fun place," commented Draven.

"The political parties met many times for peace talks, calling ceasefire after ceasefire, but nothing held longer than a few weeks. Taglen appeared to be destined for self-destruction."

Jack looked up from his tablet. "So, what happened?"

"Religion happened," replied Solo. "With the two political parties at a stalemate, a third movement rose to fill the power vacuum—a nonpartisan faction dedicated to the planet's then-undersubscribed faith worshipping the twin Goddesses of Persha and Hann."

"A holy binity," Tc'aarlat put in.

Jack's brow furrowed. "Binity?"

"Sure," said Tc'aarlat. "The Christian religion you humans brought from Earth has a holy trinity—father, son and holy ghost—and this belief system has two deities. So, a binity."

"Does it work like that?" questioned Jack. "And, more importantly, how the hell do you know this stuff?"

Tc'aarlat shrugged. "I'm smarter than I look."

Jack turned back to the viewscreen. "Thank Heaven for that."

"Actually, Heaven is a concept the Taglen religion does not have," corrected Solo. "At least, not as humans understand it."

"They don't believe in an afterlife?" Draven asked.

"In a way, Captain," replied Solo. "Taglens believe if they spend their lives following the three strict commandments laid down by the Goddess Persha, they will spend eternity in the company of her sister Hann, immersed in pure unadulterated pleasure."

"She's the fun one, then," offered Jack.

"I prefer the sound of Hann over her repressed sister," said Tc'aarlat.

Jack nodded in agreement. "And this system works?"

"It certainly appears so," replied Solo. "Taglen has been at peace for almost three decades now."

"And the moons?" said Draven.

"They are like their namesakes," explained Solo. "The Moon of Persha is home to one of the most heavily-guarded high-security prisons in the sector."

"And yet that Malfic guy broke out of there," Jack reminded them.

"He did indeed," confirmed Solo. "It is possible he may

have made for the Moon of Hann, where there are few laws. The entire moon is given over to self-gratification and fulfillment. If there is a pastime you enjoy, no matter how depraved, it can be catered to on Hann."

"Sign me up for a two-week vacation!" Tc'aarlat chuckled. "After weeks on the trail of those slave traders I could go for some sex, drugs, and Tootsie Rolls."

Draven frowned and opened his mouth to speak, but Jack raised a hand. "Best not to ask."

"What are your orders, Captain?" queried Solo.

Jack thought for a moment. "I think it would be a good idea to head for the planet rather than either of the moons. Nathan apparently suspects Malfic will still be somewhere in the local system. Taglen seems as good a place to start as any."

"We're heading for Taglen then?" Adina asked as she and Callis stepped onto the bridge. "What's the plan there?"

Jack spun to face the two women. "Go change into your Sunday best. We're heading to church!"

10

ICS Fortitude, Adina's Cabin

Adina reached into the repurposed storage locker that served as her wardrobe and took out a hangar with a short black dress.

"Try this one," she said, holding the garment up in front of Callis. "It should about be your size."

The teenager took the dress and stared at it. "I don't think so," she said, wrapping her arms around herself. "It's lovely, but I don't think it's right for me."

Adina sat on her narrow bunk and patted the blanket to indicate Callis should sit beside her.

"How long have you been wearing this thing?" she asked, gently adjusting the shoulder of her ragged dress.

Callis shrugged. "They took my clothes when I was first captured. I had a plain green dress for the first couple of years, but when I grew out of that—"

"They gave you this?" asked Adina.

"Not exactly," Callis replied. "There was another girl—Elva. She got sick and..."

The teenager fought back her tears. "I took this dress from her before they took her body away."

"Where did they take her?"

This time Callis couldn't stop the tears. "There were a handful of kids who died during the time I was there. We asked if we could bury them."

"And did they let you?"

"The first couple of times, yes. We were staying in an old abandoned cabin in the woods at the time. It was miles from anywhere and we found this little glade—just a patch of forest with fewer trees, you know? There were wildflowers growing at the edges.

"We took turns digging until the holes were deep enough, then we held hands and said a few words. We knew it wasn't a real service, but it was the best we could do."

"I'm sure it was beautiful."

"Then they took us to that warehouse in the city," Callis continued. "After that, they just took away the body of anyone who didn't make it. They didn't allow us to go with them so I don't know where they... How they..."

Adina wrapped an arm around Callis' shoulders and hugged her tightly. "You've been through so much," she murmured softly. "But you're free now, and you have to start enjoying that freedom."

Callis was silent for a moment. "I... I'm not sure I know how."

"Well," suggested Adina. "Changing your clothes is as good a place to start as any. Come with me."

She tossed the dress onto her bed, then took the girl's hand and led her out of the cabin and along the corridor to the ship's crew's bathroom.

"But first, you should take a long hot shower." She spun the dial to start the flow of water. "I'll go grab you a towel."

Moon of Hann, Blue Diamond Casino, Private Lounge

Jolio Phisk stepped out of the shower and called for one of the young females lounging on the bed in the adjoining room to hand him a towel.

"Thank you, my dear," he said, eagerly eyeing her naked frame as she wiggled back onto the bed. "I shall pray hard to the Goddess Persha for your redemption."

As always, Phisk had gotten more than his congregation's credits' worth from the casino. The girls had performed extremely well, especially the newcomer—a petite rose-scaled Snowbiral named Klarvorn. In fact, she had been so creative and enthusiastic the high priest was considering her as a permanent replacement for Chastity.

As he dried his skin he activated his tablet and brought up the remaining balance on his account.

Perfect! He had more than enough credits left to enjoy the rest of his stay. Fine food, good wine, and ample time to play the tables. He hoped to win a sizable amount to take back to the temple on Taglen. And if he didn't, so what?

It wasn't as if he were gambling with his own money.

Once he was dressed he tipped the girls and opened the door to the soundproofed room, allowing the noise of slot machines, jingling coins, and crowing croupiers to wash over him. He stood there for a moment breathing it all in.

Sometimes it was good to be a priest.

He made for the nearest card table, only to be stopped by an extremely large man in a tight-fitting suit. He was carrying a cracked leather sports bag and accompanied by a smaller companion who appeared to be dressed as a rubberized frog.

"You Gilt?" the giant rumbled, placing a huge hand on Phisk's shoulder.

The high priest glanced down at it disdainfully, but the large man did not remove it. "No, I am not," he replied, scanning the room.

"You will find Zalah Gilt over there by the bar," he added, pointing to where the floor manager was standing.

The huge figure grunted what may have been his thanks and strode over to Gilt, his lime-green sidekick scurrying after him with burning cheeks and eyes fixed firmly on the well-worn carpet.

After brushing imaginary debris from his shoulder Jolio Phisk completed his journey to the Make Twenty-Eight table, taking his seat just as the previous game came to a close.

This appeared to be a matter of dismay for one of his potential fellow gamblers, who began to shout angrily and reached across the table to where the female croupier was adding his lost chips to her tray.

"No!" he cried, lunging out with his hand. "I don't care if I went over twenty-eight! I demand to play again. I'm a valued customer, remember? I won the jackpot, for fuck's sake!"

"Mr. Quell!" snapped the croupier. "If you do not moderate your behavior I shall be forced to call security!"

Phisk spotted two burly uniformed men striding in their direction and decided to switch to a different table, making a mental note to write a sternly-worded letter to the casino's owner once he was back at home.

The Blue Diamond used to be the one establishment on Hann where one could be certain of avoiding the party-seeking vermin who perpetually flooded the moon.

If it wasn't for the quality of the girls and the thickness of the dirt on the unwashed vegetables the place provided, he'd be searching for a new sanctuary already.

"Get off me!" roared a furious voice. "Nat, get Mr. Domp for me right now! You people can't treat me like this!"

"Mr. Quell! Lowlon! Please calm down!"

Jolio Phisk rolled his eyes as the scuffle at the Make Twenty-Eight table escalated. The muscled security officers were now trying to drag the aggrieved gambler away from the croupier and her chips tray—and that brought him to a decision.

Tonight he'd be staking the temple's accumulated funds on whichever game was in the quietest area of the casino.

ICS *Fortitude,* Bridge

"What *is* that thing?" breathed Callis as she and Adina stepped onto the bridge.

Jack spun in his chair to look the two women up and down. "Hey, I said we were going to church, not some high-class fashion show!"

Her cheeks burning, the teenager tried to stop herself from smiling but failed miserably. Instead, she glanced away from the image of the vast gate filling the room's viewscreens.

"She looks great, doesn't she?" Adina smiled and Callis blushed harder. "There was a real beauty hiding beneath all those scowls."

"You don't scrub up too badly yourself," commented Draven from the navigator's seat.

Adina managed to keep her face from flushing but executed a small curtsey by way of a thank you. Having loaned her favorite dress to Callis, she had chosen a deep blue suit for herself, which she had complemented with a crisp white blouse and fashionable black shoes.

"It's just a little something I threw together." She shrugged.

"Bistok bollocks!" exclaimed Tc'aarlat. "I've never been one to get space-sick, but if you don't all stop with the soppy slushy stuff I'm going to end up smothered in regurgitated raal hawk snacks!"

SQUAAAWWW!

Mist stepped from foot to foot on her perch as she glared down at her owner, repeatedly clenching her talons.

"I think you just confessed to stealing her treats," said Adina. "And watch your language, please. We have a young person on board!"

Draven teasingly ran his fingers through his thick blond hair. "It's kind of you to say so, but I'm actually quite a bit older than I look. I think a lot of it is down to my moisturizing regime."

Callis giggled. "I don't mind, really," she said to Adina. "I heard a lot worse from the traders when they dealt with slave owners who didn't pay on time."

"That may be," said Jack, "but once we pass through this gate we have less than an hour's flight to Taglen and church."

He spun to face his Yollin copilot. "I need everyone to be on their best behavior."

"Why did you look at me when you said that?" demanded Tc'aarlat.

Jack shrugged. "I wonder..."

"There's no need to worry," countered the Yollin. "I'll be as good as mold."

Jack sighed. "The phrase is 'as good as *gold*.'"

"Gold?" queried Tc'aarlat. "As in the metal? What's good about that?"

"It's expensive," replied Adina. "And pretty."

"*Pfft!*" Tc'aarlat scoffed. "You wouldn't say that if you had grown up in a house made of the stuff."

Draven's eyes grew wide. "Wait, you grew up in a solid-gold house?"

Tc'aarlat nodded. "At least until my four-legged family decided it was too much of a scandal to keep me around. Then I was disowned and shoved off to a grotty boarding school to be savagely bullied."

"Thank goodness it didn't have any lasting effect on your personality," muttered Jack beneath his breath. "We'd better—"

"Wait," interrupted Adina. "I still want to know why Tc'aarlat thinks the human phrase is 'as good as mold.' What could possibly be good about mold?"

The Yollin's mandibles quivered with joy as he

explained, "It's the tangiest of all spices. You clearly couldn't taste the individual ingredients in the traditional Yollin stew I made last week."

"You put *mold* in our food?" Adina cried.

Tc'aarlat nodded again. "Of course! It's a rare delicacy back on Yoll, but we've got a seemingly endless supply of the stuff growing in that disused cold storage room at the rear of the fourth-floor cargo hold."

Adina clamped a hand over her mouth. "I think I'm going to puke!"

"Now you know how I feel when you lot pay each other sickeningly sweet compliments!" Tc'aarlat stated.

The three original crew members began to talk rapidly over one another.

"We need to have a talk," insisted Jack with a disgusted expression. "If you think you can just add any old shit to our food..."

"I can't believe you did that!" exclaimed Adina. "Jack and I might have been poisoned because you're happily using any old crap you stumble across as ingredients..."

"Whoa, whoa, whoa!" blurted Draven. "While I agree that everyone should be able to have their say in what they're eating..."

Callis stood near the entrance to the bridge, looking from one person to the next—and then at the viewscreens, which still showed the same stunning close-up view of the vast circular gate.

"Excuse me," she interrupted as firmly as she dared.

The row continued unabated.

She tried again a little louder.

"*Excuse me!*"

The crew kept arguing, oblivious to the teenager's attempt to catch their attention.

Finally, Callis sighed and issued a whistle so loud and shrill that everyone immediately stopped fighting and covered their ears.

SKORRRR! shrieked Mist.

Everyone turned to look at Callis.

The young girl smiled. "Has anyone else noticed that we're not moving?"

The Shadows looked at each other, then at the viewscreens.

"She's right," confirmed Jack. "Solo, why haven't you passed through the gate yet? Wait, why am I even asking that question?"

He sighed as the ship's EI frowned on the center screen.

"It's because we're not wearing our safety belts, isn't it?" asked Jack.

"The welfare of the passengers is my highest priority, Captain," explained Solo.

"Everyone buckle up or we'll be going nowhere fast," grumbled Jack, reaching for his seatbelt.

Draven stood, gesturing for Adina to return to her chair.

"Wait a minute," she exclaimed as she sat down and clicked her safety harness into place. "We're a seat short now."

Jack looked around the bridge. "We are?"

"Yes," replied Adina. "Draven had the flip-down seat earlier, but that leaves nowhere for Callis to sit."

"She can take it," Draven offered the teen the temporary chair and held it for her as she sat down. "I'll be fine."

"No," countered Tc'aarlat. "Solo won't budge unless you're strapped in."

"I will be," insisted Draven heading for the exit. "I'll sit in the pilot's seat of the *Pegasus*."

The Yollin blinked. "What?"

"The *Pegasus*," repeated Draven. "It's got seats, seatbelts —everything I need."

"Wait!" Tc'aarlat cried, trying to unbuckle his harness. "There's no need for you to go all the way down there. Here, take my seat. I'll sit in the *Pegasus* instead."

"No, it's fine," replied Draven. "I don't mind. Besides, the copilot's chair is yours."

"But you're the guest!" declared Tc'aarlat, finally unclasping the buckle and jumping up.

"And you belong on the bridge!" insisted Draven, turning to leave.

Tc'aarlat chased him. "I'm not needed up here! Really, I hardly do anything at all."

"It's still better if you're there, in case of an emergency."

"Jack can handle anything that comes up."

"Yes, but..."

Their voices faded as their footsteps rang faster and faster. It was clear to the trio on the bridge that they were both running toward the rear hangar and the sleek shuttle.

After a moment's silence Adina asked, "How long did you say the flight was on the other side of the gate?"

"Under an hour," Jack replied.

Adina turned to face the navigation control panel. "It's going to feel like an eternity."

11

Moon of Hann, Blue Diamond Casino, Main Entrance

Sergeant Randy Barber pulled his police cruiser up to the entrance of the Blue Diamond Casino and snatched up the handset of his radio.

"Dispatch, this is 5502. Arrived at the Blue Diamond Casino on Victory Boulevard. No sign of the reported disturbance, over."

The speaker set into the car's dashboard hissed static for a second, then a tinny voice responded, "Roger, 5502. The caller stated the disturbance was inside the casino at one of the Make Twenty-Eight tables, over."

Sergeant Barber smiled as he pressed the button on his handset. "Make Twenty-Eight? That was my game of choice back when I was known to place a wager or three. Tough to beat the bank, but when you did? Oh boy, over."

The dispatcher chuckled as he replied. "Well, try to control yourself when you're inside, Sarge. I don't want to have to send a second unit over to drag *you* out of there as well, over."

"I'll be good, Mike. Have to leave the car double-parked, so I'm going to light 'er up before I head in, over."

"Roger that. Do you need backup, over?"

"Nah! It'll just be some sore loser they want to eject from the premises before he upsets the other gamblers. I'll have a word with the guy, make sure he's sober enough to get back to his hotel, then head on back. Make sure you got that coffee machine on, you hear, over?"

"Will do, Sarge. Dispatch out."

Flicking the switch that would light up the blue flashing lights fixed to the roof of his vehicle, Barber climbed out of his car, pulling on his cap and tugging it down to ensure the fit was snug.

While he wasn't exactly embarrassed by his rapidly expanding bald spot, he didn't want to advertise the fact that he was increasingly follically challenged either.

There could be any number of middle-aged females in there in dire need of a little R&R after a hard evening's gambling.

Nodding politely to the sequin-clad dancers dressing the casino's main entrance, he absent-mindedly tapped his fingers against the pistol secured in the holster on his belt as he made his way inside.

Barber had been working as a cop on the Moon of Hann for over sixteen years. He'd trained at the academy and spent his first few years as a rookie on Taglen, transferring to Hann when the Temple of Persha had designated the moon as the only place in the system where the normal rules of decency didn't apply.

With hundreds of pleasure-seekers taking the short trip in search of their personal form of gratification, the need for competent officers ballooned.

Policing revelers in search of anything from home-brewed liquor and mind-bending drugs to pornographic pastimes of pure perversion required something of a gentle touch.

No good kicking down the door of a brothel specializing in providing realistic corpses in varying states of decay if you want anyone with a boner for the buried to give you their real name and home address.

Necrophiliacs, along with all other sexual deviants, had to be handled with care.

More often than not the incidents Barber was called to required only a firm hand, a pocketful of good advice, and a night in the tank to sleep off whatever was making that particular perp scream obscenities at the terrifying figments of their medicated imagination.

He enjoyed his work.

As he strode across the casino floor, he swept the gaming tables with the gaze of an experienced former gambler. He could instantly tell which customers were winning, which were losing, and which—aha!—which were vainly arguing that they have been both cheated and mistreated.

Barber's eyes narrowed as he spotted the troublemaker struggling to free himself from the grip of the venue's in-house security guards and he turned in that direction.

And that was when he felt the barrel of the gun against his temple.

Planet Taglen, Lymak City, Temple of Persha

Jack led the Shadows across a tree-lined courtyard to the steps leading up to the arched entrance of a vast white marble temple.

The flight between the gate and Taglen had been mostly uneventful, although the crew had been at a loss for words when Solo had explained that the airspace control computer on the ground had insisted they each declare their religious beliefs before it would grant permission for the *Fortitude* to land.

Both Adina and Jack professed to be lapsed followers of their respective faiths—Christianity and Hinduism, while Callis claimed to have lost all belief in a higher power after her family had sold her into slavery.

The only real shock had come when Draven openly declared himself to be a devoted disciple of a relatively new and abstract religion known as 'Transcendental Space-Buddhism,' an assertion which had led the staunchly atheistic Tc'aarlat to mutter "Now *there's* a fucking surprise!"

Once everyone's belief systems had been logged the Taglen airspace control computer had passed on the necessary flight permissions, along with precise coordinates for where Solo was to land.

A short journey on public transport later, the extended crew found themselves climbing the stairs to Lymak City's ultimate seat of power—the Temple of Persha.

"The head honcho is a guy named Jolio Phisk," Jack explained, reading from his tablet.

"Who's he, then?" inquired Tc'aarlat. "The President? Prime Minister?"

"High priest," replied Jack. "By all accounts, he's been in power ever since the planet switched from politics to religion as a means of governance."

The Yollin scowled as he gazed at the temple's towering spire. "The more I hear about this place, the less I like it."

"You can't judge other peoples' cultures," warned Draven.

"Yes I can," Tc'aarlat countered. "I did it just then. Weren't you listening, or couldn't you hear me because of your long hair?"

"I meant that you *shouldn't* judge other cultures," Draven asserted. "Just because they're not the same as yours doesn't mean they're wrong."

"Don't judge me, Draven," warned Tc'aarlat. "You know absolutely nothing about my culture."

"Yeah," scoffed Adina with a sly wink to Jack and Callis. "Tc'aarlat isn't cultured at all, are you?"

"Not in the slightest!" boasted the Yollin. "And that's exactly the way it's going to—" He stopped as the group reached the top of the stone steps, mandibles twitching as he thought back through the conversation. "Wait a second..."

As the others began to laugh, a thin man dressed in a white shirt and smart trousers ran out of the temple with an expression of anguish etched on his features.

"Please!" he cried, reaching pleadingly toward Jack. "Can you help me? They won't let me take her or even see her. I can't let them cast her into the fire; it's not right. It's my fault she's in there in the first place. I need to get her back!"

"Whoa, whoa!" Jack raised his hands in an attempt to

calm the clearly-distraught man. "It's okay. We'll help you if we can, I promise."

"What's your name?" asked Draven.

"And what's wrong?" added Adina. "You can trust us."

The teary-eyed man looked from one crew member to the next, trembling.

"I'm Corlon Strumm," he croaked, pointing to the temple entrance, "and they're about to feed my wife to the poor."

Moon of Hann, Blue Diamond Casino, Main Entrance

"Don't fucking move!" snarled Vimor Malfic.

Sergeant Barber's years of police training kicked in, so rather than turn he searched in the opposite direction, hoping to find a reflective surface in which to get a look at his aggressor.

He was in just the right spot for whoever was threatening him to be clearly visible in the glass surface of a slot machine themed after a popular brand of cheap and cheerful liquor. Barber studied him.

Oh, shit!

The man if you could call someone of that size a mere man holding a gun to his head was tall, wide, and crammed into a cheap suit that had clearly seen much better days.

The weapon appeared to be some form of blaster. If this mountain of fury were to pull the trigger it wouldn't just kill him; they'd be vacuuming fragments of his skull out of the casino's carpet for days.

Unless he could somehow wrestle it from the monster's hands.

However, the hip-level bulge under the many creases and folds in the guy's already lumpy jacket suggested he had another piece ready to go if such a miracle happened.

He was going to have to attempt to talk this bastard down.

"Hey, it's okay, buddy!" he said in as confident a voice as he could muster. "There's no need to lose your temper."

"I'll do whatever the fuck I want!" growled Malfic, thumbing off the gun's safety with a surprisingly loud click. With his other hand, he snatched Randy's gun from its holster.

"Get over there!" the felon barked, grabbing the sergeant's arm and pushing him toward the bar.

"Yeah, yeah. Sure. Whatever you say."

The cop stopped beside Nerk Wassel, taking a moment to look the kidnapped guard's lime-green rubber gimp-suit up and down.

"Hi!" said Wassel pleasantly.

By now everyone in the casino had stopped to watch the confrontation. The constant chatter had stopped, leaving only the random buzzes and bings from the various gambling machines.

Customers stared with wide eyes, their wagers temporarily forgotten.

Croupiers leaned as nonchalantly as they could against their tables, fingers searching for the panic buttons hidden underneath.

Behind the bar, the woman in a corset failed to realize the glass of wine she was pouring for a customer was already full and the extra alcohol was now spilling over the side and pooling on the wooden surface.

Malfic trained Barber's stolen weapon in his direction and swung his gun toward the bikini-clad females at the casino's main entrance.

"Close the doors!" he roared.

Two of the girls sprang into action, kicking the floor-level pads that cut the electrical current from the magnets holding the bulletproof-glass doors open.

The third bikini babe remained rooted to the spot, too scared to move. A thin trickle of urine ran down the glittering surface of her show tights.

"Lock them!" ordered Malfic. "No one gets in or out!"

One of the dancers patted the insanely small amount of her body not on view. "I don't got no keys!" she protested as bravely as she dared. "Where do you think I'd keep them, huh?"

Snorting, Malfic looked at the barmaid, who was now holding an empty wine bottle above the overflowing glass. "Who's got the keys?"

"I do," came a voice from the far end of the bar. Zalah Gilt stepped forward, unclipping a bunch of keys from his belt. "I'm the manager."

"You Gilt?" asked Malfic.

"Yeah," the manager replied, his brow furrowing. "How do you know my name?" He tossed his keys across the room and one of the dancers scurried over to where they landed in her silver high heels, returning to lock the doors as commanded.

The flashing blue lights of Sergeant Barber's car strobed against them.

"Mildew Fester told me to find you," growled Malfic to

Gilt, waving the stolen gun at the cop near the bar. "But that was before dickless here turned up to arrest me."

"What?" said Sergeant Barber. "Why would I come here to arrest you, huh? I don't even know who you are."

Malfic's finger tightened on the trigger. "Don't fucking lie!"

"I'm not!" insisted Barber. "I was called here to evict some drunken guy who was refusing to leave."

Malfic's already furious expression darkened. "Fucking liar!"

Barber raised his hands. "No, no, wait!"

Closing one eye, Vimor Malfic stiffened his arm and took aim directly at Sergeant Barber's forehead.

"It's true!" called a voice from behind the gunman.

Malfic paused and stared at Nat, who was standing behind one of the gaming tables. "It was me. I called the police to help get this guy home..."

One of the security guards lifted the obviously hammered Lowlon Quell from the carpet by the scruff of his neck, then dropped him again.

Malfic took a deep, rasping breath as he ran the situation through his mind. This pig of a cop hadn't tracked him down as an escaped prisoner at all; he'd been summoned by the casino staff to deal with a drunken customer they were having trouble ejecting.

By pulling his gun on the cop he'd given himself away, and now he was locked inside a fucking casino with dozens more hostages than just that whiny, annoying prison guard he'd grabbed to aid his getaway.

It would only be a matter of minutes before someone

came looking for the cop, then the authorities would surround this place.

And it was his own fault.

"Hey, Malfic," began the kidnapped guard, the rubber suit squeaking noisily as he took a step toward the increasingly angry escapee, "how 'bout we all sit down and work out—"

Swinging the gun in his original captive's direction, Vimor Malfic shot Nerk Wassel in the face.

12

Planet Taglen, Lymak City, Temple of Persha

Jack stared open mouthed at the trembling figure of Corlon Strumm. "Someone is going to feed your wife to the poor?! Does she get to have any say in this?"

Corlon shook his head. "She's dead!" he exclaimed. "She self-sacrificed in the temple this morning."

Adina raised her palms to calm the agitated man, "Just when you think things can't get any weirder... Why don't you back up a little and tell us everything from the beginning?"

Strumm took a deep breath and explained how his wife had been accused of blasphemy against the Goddess Persha, and as was the church's rule, had self-sacrificed in front of the entire congregation as a result.

"Wait!" said Draven. "*Self*-sacrificed?!"

Corlon Strumm nodded. "She plunged the dagger of Persha into her heart, as she was expected to do."

"*Gott Verdammt!*" cursed Tc'aarlat. "I'm the first to say

'each to his own' when it comes to religious choice, but this Persha bitch sounds like a right piss-stain!"

"*WHAT!*" Corlon Strumm's eyes rolled back in his head at Tc'aarlat's statement and he thrust out his arms in an effort to retain his balance."

"I've got you!" Jack assured him, catching the man before he fell and helping him sit down on the temple steps.

Adina sat next to him. "After your wife—"

"Merfel," said Strumm, his head in his hands.

"Merfel." Adina smiled. "After Merfel did this, what happened to her?"

Corlon wiped away his tears. "The wardens dragged her into the vestry," he explained. "Normal temple-goers aren't allowed back there, and anyone who is taken back there is never seen again. At least, not until they have been prepared for cooking."

The man's body was wracked with sobs.

"I shouldn't have told him!" he wailed. "I should have kept quiet about what she said at home. I loved her, and it's my fault she's going to be eaten by tramps and hobos!"

Adina rubbed her hand across Corlon's back and looked at the rest of the group, unsure what she should say next.

"Go home," Jack told the bereaved husband, "but leave us the details of where we can find you. We promise to return your wife's body to you."

"We do?" asked Tc'aarlat, his mandibles widening with surprise.

"We do," Jack insisted.

Corlon Strumm wiped the back of his hand across his

eyes and stood as Draven pulled out his tablet to note his contact details.

The group watched as the lone figure made his way down the temple steps and across the expanse of the tree-lined courtyard.

"He looks so lost," Callis remarked. "So alone."

"Not anymore," said Jack, turning to face the vast wooden doorway of the temple. "No one is alone when they have the Shadows on their side."

SKORRRR! shrieked Mist from her spot on Tc'aarlat's shoulder.

"While I agree with your sentiment," the Yollin put in, "don't we have an escaped convict to locate?"

"I haven't forgotten about him," Jack assured him. "I just want to have a bit of a chat with whoever's in charge."

With that he led the group up to the wooden door, selected a spot which wasn't adorned with ornate iron symbols, and hammered on it with his fist.

After a moment, the group heard a loud metallic *WHIRRR* as an ancient locking mechanism was activated. Adina glanced at the exterior part of the lock—a fist-sized metal dial with dozens of short black lines radiating outwards from the keyhole.

After a moment, the door opened just wide enough for a dark-haired man in the traditional white warden's robes to peer out.

"What!"

Jack feigned surprise. "That wasn't a particularly spiritual greeting!"

The warden blinked, clearly annoyed by Jack's presence. "Praise be to the Goddess Persha," he intoned. "Now, what do you want?!

"Not 'what,'" replied Jack. "Who or, more accurately, *whom* do I want."

The warden blinked again. "What?"

"Whom!" Jack repeated. "As in—it's a person we want, not a thing. We're here for the body of the late Merfel Strumm."

If the warden was taken aback at the name he didn't let it show in his expression.

"Who?"

"*Whom!*" Jack reiterated firmly. "You need to work on your grammar, sunshine. And you know exactly who I mean, so open this door before I personally send you for a one-on-one chat with your precious goddess."

"Fuck off!" snarled the warden and slammed the temple door.

Jack turned to the others as the lock cycled again and cracked his knuckles. "Well, he can't say I didn't warn him."

Adina crouched before the door's exterior lock. "Draven," she began as she examined it. "Why don't you and Tc'aarlat go round the back and see if you can find another way inside?"

"Er, okay," responded Draven. "Sure. If that's what you want."

Adina smiled up at him. "It would mean a lot to me," she assured him soothingly.

"Then I'm on my way!" Draven exclaimed, heading toward what appeared to be an alley running the length of the temple's far side. "With me, bird dude!"

"*What* did you call me?" cried Tc'aarlat as he dashed

after the pilot. Mist gave a *cawww* and flapped her wings as she clung tightly to his leather shoulder pad. "I'm pretty sure I outrank whatever pathetic little position you think you hold on this team, so you'd better start showing some respect, mister!"

When the two men had disappeared around the corner, Adina resumed her inspection of the lock.

"Did you just play Draven?" Jack asked with a wry smile.

Callis giggled and Adina shrugged. "I didn't want him to watch me while I work."

Standing, she took hold of Callis' shoulders and spoke earnestly. "I don't want you to be scared by what you're about to see. I don't share this secret with just anyone, but I trust you. I'm a werewolf, but I suppress it, so my Were senses aren't what they could be. I can partially change into a Were and gain those abilities, a benefit of the drugs, but it hurts. A lot."

Adina nodded to Jack, who gently pulled Callis back a few paces. Then she closed her eyes and concentrated hard.

Deep within her body, long-suppressed strands in Adina's DNA began to stir. One by one little-used areas of her brain lit up, sending urgent messages throughout her nervous system at lightning speed.

Slowly, painfully, Adina's head reshaped itself.

The teen stared aghast as her new friend tossed her head back and cried out in agony. While a Wechselbalg's transformation was normally pain-free, Adina had found that forcing her body to work against the powerful DNA suppressants was a tortuous process.

She just had to believe that the end result was worth the discomfort and anguish.

Adina grimaced as her ears elongated and moved toward the top of her skull, brownish-red strands of fur sprouting from her normally smooth skin.

A few moments later the partial transformation was complete. Adina, bending over double and gasping as she tried to catch her breath, looked just as human as she had before—except for the wolf ears standing proudly from her scalp.

"Wow!" cried Callis.

"Hey, not so loud!" begged Adina, covering her new ears with her palms. "These things are really sensitive!"

"Sorry!" came the whispered reply.

"I've seen this type of lock before," Adina explained as she knelt in front of the temple door again. "It's a modern version of those old-time twisty-turny locks they used on bank safes back on Earth. If you know the combination you can open it by moving the dial back and forth."

"And if you *don't* know the combination?" asked Jack.

Adina grinned, which was a little disconcerting when her lupine ears pricked up to accompany the expression. "Then you listen for the clicks..." she said as she pressed one of her new ears to the wooden door.

Grasping the dial, she began to turn it in a clockwise direction, slowly and listening carefully to each of the tiny clicks it made as the pointer passed from one marker to the next.

When she heard a click that sounded different to her enhanced wolf hearing, she switched direction and moved the dial carefully counter-clockwise.

Jack was reminded of an old black-and-white movie he'd seen as a kid where a team of bank robbers stood by impatiently as an aged safecracker worked his magic on the bank vault's lock.

Adina turned the wheel back and forth half a dozen times, pausing once or twice to wipe the perspiration from her hand before moving on.

Eventually she stood, brushing dirt from her skirt.

"That's it," she said to Jack. "All you have to do is spin the wheel to the right and you're in."

"OK," Jack replied. "You two hang back for a moment while I make sure there isn't some kind of unpleasant welcoming party on the other side of the door.

Adina took Callis' arm and led her away, wincing as her wolf ears reverted and returned to their human form.

Jack took a deep breath, then in one swift movement he turned the dial and pressed his shoulder against the thick wood.

There was an eerie *creeeaaak* as the door swung slowly inwards, quickly drowned out by the voice of the warden they had previously encountered.

"Hey! I told you lot to fu—"

The man's words were cut short by Jack's fist punching him squarely on the jaw. He crumpled to the hard floor, out cold.

"I can't be sure," Jack smiled at Adina and Callis, "but I *think* he just invited us inside!"

Moon of Hann, Police Headquarters, Chief's Office

Police Chief Bis Pargo took a step back and peered over the top of his half-moon glasses at the two blown-up photographs of himself being held up on the opposite side of the room.

"Neither of them!" he barked. "Neither of those screams, 'Hey, I'm a standup guy. Vote for me as the next Mayor of Hann!'"

Grumbling, he sat down and flipped open a polished wooden box on his desk, rummaging inside for one of his more expensive cigars.

Oxbo Lake set both photographs down on the room's small meeting table and scampered over to the desk, smoothing his bleached-blond goatee with tattooed fingers.

"If I may speak freely as your campaign chairperson, sir, that's *exactly* what both of those pictures scream. They're saying 'you can trust me, I'm just like you!'"

"You can see my bald spot in them!" thundered Pargo. "I gave you strict instructions to airbrush that out!"

Lake sighed as he removed his red-framed spectacles and pinched the bridge of his nose. "And I told you, sir, you're campaigning on a promise of honesty! You've called out the current Mayor on his history of lies and corruption, but you can't keep doing that if you fudge the way you look on your flyers!"

Finally locating the cigar he was searching for, Pargo snipped off the end and sat back. He pulled a matchbook emblazoned with the phrase 'Vote Pargo' on the cover from a glass bowl.

"I don't care what you told me!" the police chief rumbled. "Folks can't vote for me if they're doubled over laughing at my comb-over! I want a full head of hair on my official photograph."

"The people of Hann know that's not authentic, sir!"

"Remember where we are, Lake!" countered Pargo angrily. "Nibble my nutsack, man. If you think the disturbed fuckers who visit this vile wanton lump of rock are perverts and pissheads, you should see the six-fingered shitehawks who choose to live here! They want authenticity about as much as they want a fresh set of clothes and a job interview."

"But..."

"No buts, son! You're fired! And tell whoever replaces you that the next time I see a photograph of myself to be used in the race for mayor of this dump I expect it to have more hair than a witch's minge!"

Oxbo Lake turned to gather up the eschewed images and stuff them back into an oversized leather pouch, inwardly cursing the day he'd chosen politics over sociology as his college major. He should have ignored the cute smile of the guy behind the recruiting desk.

As he was zipping the pouch closed the office door burst open and a red-faced desk sergeant charged in.

"Chief Pargo, sir!" he blustered. "We got ourselves a hostage situation down at the Blue Diamond Casino. Some nasty bastard started shootin' up the place, and now he's locked the doors and won't let anyone in or out!"

Pargo held the flame of the match he had just struck on inch from the tip of his cigar. Pushing the stogie to the side of his mouth with his pock-marked tongue, he scowled at the out-of-breath officer.

"So? We got a hostage negotiator on the payroll, don't we?"

The sergeant nodded. "Yes sir, we do. Some fella name of Tarbuck."

"Then what're you waitin' for? Get him down there so he can talk this turd-taster into givin' himself up!"

"Yes, sir!" barked the sergeant, saluting sharply. "Right away, sir!"

Nodding to himself, Pargo rolled his cigar back to the center of his mouth and lit it.

"Well, that's a shame," commented Oxbo Lake as he made for the exit. "Real shame."

Pargo narrowed his eyes.

"What is?"

Lake turned. "Oh, nothing," he said with a small shrug. "It's just that seeing you talk down some crazed hostage-taker in person would have played real well on the midnight news bulletin. Could have been great for the campaign. But I'm fired, so I guess you don't need my advice any longer. I'll bid you good night."

Bis Pargo's cigar twitched as his face spread into a wide smile.

"Son, consider yourself rehired!"

Planet Taglen, Lymak City, Temple of Persha

Jack paused to zip-tie the unconscious warden's wrists and ankles before the group proceeded.

"I'm guessing this guy's not alone," he warned as they moved down the central aisle. "Stay sharp and keep the noise to a minimum."

SKARRRRR!

Mist's cry echoed crazily off the white marble walls, floor, and arched ceiling, causing Adina, Jack, and Callis to hastily cover their ears.

"You two are back, then?" asked Adina flatly, turning to find Tc'aarlat and Draven approaching between the empty benches.

"We were coming back to break the bad news that there was no other way inside," Draven told her, "but I see you've got that part covered."

"How did you manage to get in?" questioned Tc'aarlat.

Adina shrugged. "I just played it by ear."

"So what's the plan?" the Yollin asked.

"Well, I was going to suggest we search the place in silence," Jack replied, "but Mist pissed all over that idea."

"Hey!" explained Tc'aarlat, reaching up to scratch the raal hawk on the blood-red feathers of her chest. "It's not her fault if we're finally doing something more exciting than picking up strays."

He turned to smile at Callis. "No offense."

"None taken," replied Draven.

"I wasn't talking to you."

Jack approached the altar at the far end of the vast room. "The guy we're looking for is the high priest, Jolio Phisk," he informed them, examining the various items laid out on the bright white cloth covering the marble slab.

"And that guy's wife," Tc'aarlat reminded them, peering around the pillars toward a row of doors on a side wall. "Or rather, her mortal remains."

Taking a step backward, the Yollin bumped into a marble statue of a beautiful woman rising naked from a billowing cloud.

"Gerroff!" he yelled, flinging out a fist as he spun on the figure he presumed was attacking him. There was a crunch as his knuckles collided with solid stone.

"MOTHERFUCKING COCK-GOBBLING TWAT-PANTS!" he bellowed, shaking his hand and hopping around the base of the statue.

Jack sighed. "I always said he could start a fight in an empty church."

"Hey, it's not my fault!" Tc'aarlat growled. "She snuck up on me!"

"Yeah, she looks like one of those stealth statues I've heard so much about," commented Adina.

CLICK!

The team spun as the door beside the altar closed.

"Vestry," said Draven, reading the sign on the door as the group hurried over to the door. "I don't know a lot about churches, but I'm guessing that's where they keep the vestments."

"And where there are vestments there are priests," added Jack.

"Including at least one who knows we're here," Adina pointed out.

Jack pulled his modified Jean Dukes Special from its holster. "I'm setting this to stun," he told them, spinning the dial to three.

"They can do that now?" asked Draven.

Jack nodded. "Adina worked in Jean's lab on Base Station 11," he explained. "She knew we wanted a non-lethal option and got permission from the very top to modify them for us."

Draven gave Adina one of his more dazzling smiles and crooned, "Smart as well as beautiful!"

Producing her own Special, she waved it in Draven's direction. "And more than capable of knocking your ass out cold if you carry on with that patronizing shit."

Draven raised his hands in surrender. "Message received and understood, m'lady!"

Jack took a few steps back from the door. "Stick with Adina," he said to Callis, "and if it all goes cockeyed, get down and stay down."

The teenager nodded as Adina took her hand.

"Okay," said Jack, turning his left shoulder to the door. "On three. One... two..."

"Wait a minute!" interrupted Tc'aarlat, striding over to Jack. "If you want a door broken down you're gonna need an expert."

Jack sighed. "May I remind you that you just lost a fist fight with a statue?"

The Yollin jerked a thumb over his shoulder at the sculpture. "That's not just any statue. That's the Goddess Persha."

Jack paused, waiting for more, but it didn't come.

"So?"

"I don't hit women!" explained Tc'aarlat, his mandibles crossing. "Especially ones with rockin' bods like the groovy goddess over there."

Callis glanced at the naked statue. "Ew!"

The Yollin flexed his arms. "I save the tough stuff for opponents with a little more masculinity."

"Such as doors..." offered Adina.

"Exactly!" Tc'aarlat beamed, entirely missing the sarcasm in her voice.

"Don't forget what happened last time you tried this back on Alma Nine."

Tc'aarlat shuddered, his mandibles uncrossing and spreading wide. The Yollin had attempted to break open an apartment door, only to find it was made of some rein-forced shoulder-shattering material.

"What are the odds of that happening again?" he demanded.

Adina raised her hand. "I'll take a piece of that action!"

Ignoring her, Tc'aarlat rested the hand that wasn't

throbbing with pain on Jack's shoulder and moved him a few steps to his left.

"Stand aside," he said firmly. He twitched his shoulder, sending Mist flapping into the air. The hawk landed on the nearest bench and watched the proceedings with interest.

"Ready when you are," said Jack with a smile.

Tc'aarlat closed his eyes for a second, muttering some unheard words of self-inspiration, then took a deep breath and charged.

His shoulder was just about to make contact with the vestry door when it was flung open by a short man wielding a golden dagger.

"I don't know what you people think you're—" he managed to yell before Tc'aarlat slammed into him, sending them both crashing to the floor in the brightly-lit room beyond.

Moon of Hann, Blue Diamond Casino

"Everybody get down on the floor and shut up!"

Vimor Malfic swept his gun across the breadth of the casino as staff and customers trudged over to the bar, the only area of the establishment free of gaming tables and machines.

"You!" he spat at one of the male croupiers. "Get a box and collect everyone's communication devices. Phones, tablets, radios—the lot. If I find out any one of you has held out you'll wish you were never born!"

All told, Malfic reckoned he had at least fifty hostages. Minus one, of course, since the two security guards had asked for permission to move Nerk Wassel's body into the back room of the bar where it would be out of sight.

Fifty hostages.

Malfic sneered at his prisoners as they begrudgingly sat on the time-worn bar-area carpet, making certain to aim his weapon at anyone who looked as though they might cause trouble.

This wasn't going to be easy.

Fifty hostages.

Fifty hostages who hadn't yet worked out that together they could most likely overpower him. And the ones who had were likely to be the do-good types who weren't prepared to sacrifice their fellow captives as they mounted an attack.

Never having used the type of gun Mildew Fester had provided, he didn't know how long the charge would last or whether the ion-pulse firing mechanism required time to reset between volleys.

Even if he managed to take out eight or nine of these pathetic little fuckers, there was every chance those following would be more successful in their attack.

While there was bound to be at least one or two of these money-hungry peasants with a lower-than-acceptable level of morality, he could only hope the overall standard of integrity remained high enough to keep him safe from reprisal.

Pussies!

"*QUIET!*" he roared, all too aware that chatter could easily disguise small groups of insurgents planning to overpower him.

Malfic cursed himself for not thinking of bringing

another prisoner with him during the breakout. While adding an extra body to the plan would have been risky, at least he would have had someone to help corral these fools.

He forced the self-criticism from his mind. He had to concentrate; had to stand firm and ensure he stayed in charge.

The group of hostages fell silent, aside from the rasping sobs of some of the more pitiful punters.

By now the entire room was lit by the banks of flashing blue lights from the police cars in the street outside. Malfic knew there would also be armed cops ready at the rear of the building, and quite probably a team on the roof, too.

He was surrounded.

"Fuck!" he spat, taking two angry paces and turning to stomp back again. "*FUCK!*"

"Hey, chill out, guy!" whined one of the bargaining chips near the front of the group. "There's no need to lose your cool."

Malfic spun on him, thumbing back the hammer on his gun as his finger tightened against the trigger.

The group gasped as one. Most of them had seen this madman dispatch his partner—the guy in the green gimp suit. If this psycho was unhinged enough to kill his only ally, surely he wouldn't hesitate when it came to murdering one of the hostages.

"Don't do it," advised a calm voice from the rear of the group.

Malfic looked up to see Sergeant Barber looking right at him. The police officer shook his head slightly.

"You don't want to make things worse for yourself."

Malfic almost laughed. *Worse? How could things be any fucking worse?*

Still, the pig had a point. If he was to execute one of these dickless douche-flutes this early in the stand-off, he might as well go ahead and slaughter them all.

And that would leave the authorities with no reason not to storm the place and splash his brains from here to the fiery pits of Hell.

"Just stay calm," continued Barber. "I'm sure whoever has taken charge outside will be in contact soon, and you can negotiate your way out of here without anyone else getting hurt."

Maintaining eye contact with Barber, Malfic pushed the hammer back in place and slowly lowered his weapon.

Which was when the voice rang out.

"Hey, fuckwad! This is Chief of Police Bis Pargo and I'm giving you ten minutes to release those hostages before I order my men to come in there, rip your balls off, and stuff them down your goddamn throat, you hear?!"

As Malfic squinted out through the casino doors Sergeant Barber closed his eyes and let out a long sigh.

"Well, that's it," he muttered. "We're all dead."

Planet Taglen, Lymak City, Temple of Persha

Dabriel Yagash blinked as he came around, trying extremely hard to banish whoever was using the inside of his skull as a steel drum.

"He's back with us," announced a female voice.

The blurry figure of someone he didn't recognize

stepped aside, allowing someone else he didn't recognize to take their place.

Where in the name of Persha was he? And who were these people?

People...

Oh my!

Dabriel's eyes snapped wide open as the memory pounded home. There had been a group of strange-looking people attacking the temple, and when he'd tried to protect the church and its holy treasures from the invaders the ugliest among them had run straight at him and knocked him over.

Panicked, he tried to jump to his feet, but only succeeded in slipping off the bench where the attackers had seated him and falling to the floor.

His eyes grew wider as he realized that his hands and feet were bound together with some type of plastic strip.

"Wh-what do you want?!" he stammered, looking from one face to another. "If you try to cause me harm the Goddess Persha will protect me!"

"Persha can kiss my crusty Yollin ass!" growled one of the interlopers.

It was the ugly one again!

"Sinner!" squealed Dabriel, struggling to wiggle toward the door on his bottom.

Another of the gang of raiders placed a hand on his shoulder to hold him still. "We're not going to hurt you," he insisted.

"I'm already hurt!" protested Dabriel, nodding to Tc'aar-lat. "The ugly one hurt me!"

"Hey, Draven, he's talking about you!"

"No," protested Dabriel. "I meant you!"

"Ha!"

"Shut the fuck up, Draven!"

"Make me..."

"I fucking will, you rat bastard. Just name the time and place."

"Quiet!" bellowed the gate-crasher holding Dabriel in place. "That was an accident," he said in a much kinder voice than the others were using. "We're sorry about that. We just want some information."

"And a body," said Tc'aarlat over Jack's shoulder. "Don't forget to ask him about the body."

"I won't forge—" Jack sighed. "Are you going to let me do this, or do you want to take over? No, don't answer that! Just go outside and check that there are no more of those white-robed ass-baskets out there."

"Why me?" barked the Yollin. "Why can't Draven check?"

"Both of you go!" yelled Jack, finally losing his cool. "Now!"

Grumbling, Tc'aarlat stomped to the door and out into the main area of the temple, Draven at his heels.

"Now," said Jack, turning back to Dabriel, "I'm going to cut you free, but I need your promise that you won't try to do anything silly, okay?"

The stocky man nodded.

With one hand, Jack grabbed the cable-tie holding Dabriel's feet together, and reached out to the two women behind him with the other. The taller of the two handed him a knife.

But not just any knife.

It was a golden dagger.

The Dagger of Persha!

The Dagger of Persha that must not under ANY circumstances be handled by anyone other than a priest of the temple or a self-sacrificing sinner, lest the Goddess herself return to Taglen to smite whomsoever should have been protecting such an important relic.

And HE was that failed protector!

Dabriel's terrified eyes rolled back in his head as he lapsed into unconsciousness once more.

14

Planet Taglen, Lymak City, Temple of Persha

The second time Dabriel Yagash regained consciousness that day he was surprised to find himself sitting in a
chair but not strapped to it.

He glanced at the door leading to the main area of the
temple, but found the potential exit blocked by the two
aliens who had been bickering with each other earlier.

Two women stood before the opposite door, rendering
that an unlikely choice for escape.

That left the final alien—the male who appeared to be
in charge of the group. He was sitting in the chair opposite
Dabriel's, watching him with interest as he shook his head
to clear the fuzziness.

"How are you feeling?" the alien inquired.

"My head hurts," replied Dabriel.

"Here," said Jack, holding out a glass of clear liquid.

Dabriel eyed the offering suspiciously.

"It's just water," Jack assured Dabriel, taking a sip himself. "It will make you feel better."

Nervous, Dabriel accepted the glass, but after a few mouthfuls he had to admit his interrogator had been correct. It *did* make him feel better.

"Thank you," he said, setting the glass on the floor beside his chair.

"No problem." Jack smiled. "Now, if you don't mind, we have a couple of questions we'd like to ask you, Mr. Phisk."

"Wait!" cried Dabriel, holding up a hand. "You think I'm Jolio Phisk?"

Jack nodded, glancing at the taller of the two women who simply shrugged in response. "Are you telling me you *aren't* Phisk?"

"Of course I'm not," exclaimed Dabriel. "He's high priest of the Temple of Persha. I don't compare to him in any way, shape, or form."

"Whoa, there's a tightly knotted complex for some lucky therapist to unravel," commented Tc'aarlat.

"Where *is* Phisk?" asked Jack, drawing Dabriel's attention back to himself.

"I... I don't know," replied the deputy high priest. "But he's not here."

"We know that," asserted Draven. "We searched the place from top to bottom while you were taking your nap."

"Here's the thing," said Jack, edging his chair just a little closer to Dabriel's. "I think you *do* know where Jolio Phisk is right now, and you're going to tell us."

"I don't, and I won't," Dabriel insisted. "I can't!"

Jack sighed, looking up at his colleagues once again.

None of them had anything to say.

Jack edged even closer to the apprehensive priest.

"Have you heard of the Etheric Federation?"

Dabriel's brow knitted for a second. "Yes," he replied, clearly not expecting this change of direction in the questioning. "Everyone has."

"Okay," said Jack. "Now, we are official representatives of the Federation, and it would only take one quick call to bring a metric ton of *Etheric* shit down on you and this entire temple. And, trust me, you do *not* want to be the person responsible for that."

"They would tear this place apart," agreed Adina. "All they need is the tiniest hint that your religion isn't a hundred percent legit or moral—y'know, such as making members of the public commit suicide and then cooking their corpses for tramp food—and they'd have entire teams of nasty bastards crawling all over this temple. And if they were to find something, *anything* they didn't like the look of..."

Instead of finishing the sentence, Adina simply widened her eyes and let out a long, dramatic breath.

"I've seen them at work," added Tc'aarlat, "and let me tell you, buddy, I wouldn't want these nosy sonsofbitches going through *my* past."

"Although to be fair, you'd be unlikely to remember it if they *did* discover something unpleasant about you," continued Draven. "Hell, you'd be hard-pressed to remember your own damn name by the time they'd finished with you. And you sure as hell wouldn't be waking up on this poxy planet."

"Please!" begged Dabriel, his eyes wide with fear. "You mustn't. Phisk..."

"Is the guy we really want to question," finished Jack, "so just tell us where he is and we can make all this unpleasantness go away."

Dabriel lowered his head for a moment. When he raised it again he wore a different expression. One of defiance.

"I don't care what happens to me," he announced firmly. "So go ahead—call your Federation friends. I'm not saying another word."

"All right," said Jack with a sigh as he pulled his tablet from inside his jacket. "But, don't say we didn't warn you."

"Wait!" said Adina, crossing to crouch beside Dabriel's chair. She rested a hand on his forearm. "You say you don't care what happens to you, because you *do* care what happens to someone else. Who is it?"

"What?" spluttered Dabriel. "You... I mean... No! I don't know what you're talking about!"

Draven approached Dabriel's chair from the other side. "Adina's right, isn't she? You won't talk because you're afraid that if you do, Phisk will target somebody you care for."

Tears flooded Dabriel's eyes.

"My daughter, Hamble" he croaked. "He's always promised that if I were ever to disclose any of his secrets he'd kill her."

"I'm sorry to hear that," said Jack, sliding his tablet away.

Dabriel nodded his thanks but kept his gaze lowered.

"As horrible as that threat is, I've finally heard one thing about this wacko religion I like," said Adina. "In many other cultures priests are forbidden from marrying and having families. Some even insist on total abstinence from sexual contact."

"It's the same here," said Dabriel, drying his eyes. "I met Jemima not long after I graduated from the seminary. We both knew what we were doing made us sinners, but we couldn't stop."

Adina squeezed his arm. "And then Hamble came along?"

Dabriel nodded. "Phisk promoted me to this office as soon as he found out about her."

"You couldn't keep her a secret from him?" Tc'aarlat inquired.

The deputy high priest closed his eyes before answering. "Jemima died in childbirth. I wanted her to go to the hospital, but she was so scared about what would happen if one of the doctors was to contact Phisk that she stayed home. There were complications, and..."

The rest of Dabriel's explanation faded away.

"If I help you in any way Phisk will declare us both sinners. Me for engaging in a relationship, and Hamble for being born out of wedlock. He will make us both self-sacrifice."

"Not if we protect you," Jack assured him.

Despite his tears Dabriel almost laughed. "From Phisk? You clearly don't know him very well. He owns this planet now. He can do just about anything he likes. There's no way you could protect us."

All eyes turned to Callis as she stepped forward. Adina stood and moved back, allowing the teenager to take her place at Dabriel's side.

"I know you're scared," she told him. "I was too, for such

a long time. I was kidnapped by some very bad men. Bad men who hurt me and murdered my friends. Then these guys showed up and saved all of us."

Dabriel looked at Callis as she talked.

"They saved me when I thought it couldn't happen. When I thought I would spend whatever short life I had left in constant fear and pain."

Callis smiled and took Dabriel's hand.

"If anyone can protect you and your daughter, it's them."

Dabriel looked from Callis to Jack and wiped the tears from his eyes before taking a long, deep breath.

"Jolio Phisk is at the Blue Diamond Casino on the Moon of Hann!"

Moon of Hann, Blue Diamond Casino

Oxbo Lake shot out a hand, grabbing Chief Bis Pargo's wrist before he could raise the megaphone to his mouth again.

"Sir, I know that you choosing to handle the negotiations yourself was my idea, but I wonder if I may suggest allowing the officer with training for these scenarios to take charge?"

Pargo scowled. "Why?"

"Because I doubt yelling at the suspect that you're going to *'shove a red-hot poker right up his chocolate starfish'* is not likely to result in a peaceful solution to this siege."

"I agree!" barked a tall figure beside Lake.

"And who the fuck might you be?" demanded the police chief.

"I'm Chan Peel," said the man. "The department's trained negotiator."

"Didn't I send word that you should stand down?"

"Yes sir, you did."

"Then why are you here?"

"Because I didn't think you were serious, sir."

"Of course I was serious!" snapped Pargo. "Imagine the publicity when those hostages are brought out because of me!"

"Even if they're brought out in body bags?" asked Peel.

Oxbo Lake buried his face in his hands.

"If the shitdick behind this is in one of those bags I still see it as a win," asserted Pargo. "I'll come out of this as tough on crime—exactly what's needed to be mayor of this craphole. Now sod off before I demote you to..."

He turned to his publicist. "What's a really shitty job?"

Lake shrugged. "Right now, sir? Mine."

"Fair enough," growled Pargo, switching his gaze to Chan Peel. "Sod off before I give you *his* job!"

As the negotiator wandered away, cursing under his breath, Pargo once again snatched up the megaphone.

"Please, sir," begged Lake. "At least *try* to be considerate. There are lives at stake here as well as votes."

Pargo sighed. "Very well."

He raised the megaphone to his mouth.

"You in there! What do you want? What are your demands?"

He paused, continuing just before Lake was about to point out that he shouldn't expect an immediate response.

"Whatever they are, I won't even listen until you make a gesture of goodwill and release those hostages!"

Inside the casino, Jolio Phisk sat silently among his fellow captives, working out which of them would be useful as a living shield should the police storm the building and a gun battle ensue.

Vimor Malfic paced up and down a short distance away, cursing his luck and desperately trying to devise an escape plan.

As Chief Pargo's latest communication echoed around the room, he looked at the doors and snarled.

Stupid pig! As if he'd even consider going along with that idea. If he freed the hostages he'd have nothing left to bargain with. The cops would use him for target practice and not stop until he was so dead his ancestors felt it.

However, if he were to release *some* of the hostages—no, *most* of them—that would even out the numbers a little. Give him fewer potential have-a-go heroes to worry about and make that gesture of goodwill Chief Fucker McFuckface was yelling about.

Ha! The pig in charge had just given him the perfect answer to his most immediate problem.

"Listen up!" Malfic yelled, spinning on the hostages. "You, you, and you!" he said, pointing at Lowlon Quell, Nat, and one of the entrance greeters with his gun. "Get over there by the change machine!"

"Why?" demanded the bikini babe. "What are you going to do with us?"

"Just do it!"

Looking nervously at the other hostages, Nat helped Quell to his feet and helped him to stagger shakily over to the spot their captor had indicated. The greeter, Deedee

Joh, followed, making the effort to glare at Malfic all the way.

Next the villain gestured to Zalah Gilt. "Who's the big boss here?" he demanded. "Who's in charge?"

Gilt climbed to his feet. "I'm the manager..."

"Like I give a fuck!" Malfic sneered. "They're not going to leave a thin streak of piss like you in command of a turdpit like this."

"It's me," announced Thavo Domp, using the edge of the bar to hoist himself up. "I'm Thavo Domp, owner of this 'turdpit'."

"Over there!" ordered Malfic. "Both of you!"

The two men joined the three hostages already separated from the rest of the group. Thavo Domp put his arm around Nat's shoulders and gave her a reassuring squeeze.

"OK," snarled Malfic. "Now the cop, and the smug bastard sitting next to you. Go!"

Sergeant Barber turned to the lean figure beside him- Jolio Phisk.

"We'd better do as he wants," advised Barber, taking care not to step on anyone's fingers or toes as he picked his way through the group.

Working hard to maintain an air of importance, Phisk did the same.

Vimor Malfic's lips moved as he silently counted the people he had chosen to keep as his insurance against an immediate and violent end to the stand-off, then turned to the remaining hostages.

"The rest of you, get the fuck out!"

A wave of relief swept across the room as those remaining

in the bar area cautiously stood and hurried toward the main doors, all the while keeping a close eye on the villain's weapon just in case this was some kind of cruel prank.

Would their captor really give them the hope of release only to gun them down as they made their way to freedom?

"Gilt!" Malfic shouted to those chosen to remain. "Let them out, then lock the door behind them."

Nodding, Gilt joined the exodus, pulling a large bunch of keys from his trouser pocket.

But he wasn't the only one on the move.

Jolio Phisk found himself the recipient of an angry snarl as he made his way over to Malfic.

"What the fuck do you think you're doing, cumnugget?"

Phisk did his best to remain stoic. "It would be in your best interests to release me as well."

A look of thunder spread across Malfic's face. "Is that so?" he growled, pulling back the hammer on his gun once more.

"Yes," replied Phisk. "Swap me for one of those window-lickers before they all leave."

"And exactly why would I do that?"

"It would demonstrate a certain intelligence," Phisk explained. "That you're not just some dumb fuck who somehow managed to find his way off the moron farm."

Snarling, Malfic quickly raised his gun and pressed the barrel into the dead center of this mutinous jerk's forehead.

"Go ahead!" he hissed. "Keep up with the insults, shit-for-brains. I fucking dare you!"

Phisk didn't flinch. "You wouldn't say that if you had the slightest idea who you were talking to."

"Is that correct?"

"Absolutely."

Vimor Malfic turned his weapon ninety degrees to the left, the muzzle pressing a circular indentation into Phisk's pale skin.

"OK, I'll humor you," growled Malfic. "*Then* I'll blow your goddamn brains out the back of your skull. Who are you?"

"I am Jolio Phisk," came the confident reply. "High priest of the Temple of Persha and chosen mouthpiece of the twin goddesses."

Malfic considered this information for a moment.

"I understand you will be feeling foolish right now," asserted Phisk, using the back of his hand to push the aggressor's gun away from his face. "However, I agree not to share with the authorities your blunder in keeping me behind once I have been liberated."

Vimor Malfic smiled darkly. "That is very kind of you."

"Think nothing of it."

"So you're the infamous Jolio Phisk, huh?"

"The very same."

"The high priest?"

"Just that."

"Nah, you're more than just a high priest," Malfic countered.

Phisk frowned. "I am?"

"Yeah!"

"I don't understand," Phisk confessed. "What am I?"

This time Malfic grinned. "You're my fucking trump card, dude!"

Pulling back his hand, the felon slammed the handle of his gun as hard as he could into the high priest's face and turned Jolio Phisk's world into an all-consuming sea of darkness.

15

Moon of Hann, The Barbed Codpiece S&M Dungeon

In their makeshift base of operations, Chief Pargo walked the long line of police officers taking statements from dozens of recently-released casino hostages.

Pargo had originally wanted to set up shop in the Shrillexian Fusion Restaurant directly opposite the Blue Diamond Casino. However the maitre'd had not been happy at the prospect of losing an entire evening's business from a long line of well-paying customers—some of whom had booked months in advance for the opportunity to sample the celebrity chef's much-praised experimental cuisine.

Instead, the team had been forced to requisition the business next door to the restaurant as their temporary headquarters, where fewer customers would be inconvenienced.

The Barbed Codpiece S&M Dungeon catered to an extremely different type of clientele. It was a legal brothel specializing in discreet sado-masochistic experiences for visitors with a taste for leather, chains, whips, and oddly-shaped vibrating devices designed to be used in any number of oddly-shaped alien orifices.

Following the promise of a full refund and free upgrade to gold-plated nipple clamps upon their next visit, the dungeon's patrons and dedicated staff had vacated the premises, leaving the police department free to occupy the business's popular Pit of Pain and convert it into a fully-functioning ops area.

Currently just over a dozen of the casino's freshly-freed hostages were perched on a wide variety of discomfort-delivering devices as they gave first-hand witness accounts of what had happened to them across the street.

Several of the grateful gamblers were already raising the question of compensation from the casino's owner, and one particularly perturbed punter was loudly demanding the chance to return to the scene of the crime to retrieve the stack of chips he had been forced to leave behind.

Whenever the opportunity arose, the opportunistic police chief would pause beside one of the distraught witnesses to insist they accept a Pargo for Mayor button from him or ensure they listened to pre-prepared sound-bites disparaging his rival's utter lack of decency.

All the while wielding a sleek ebony dildo he had confiscated from one of the establishment's 'insertion experts,' which he believed to be a shiny version of the standard-issue police nightstick.

Pargo still couldn't work out exactly what benefit the vibrate function would provide when cops used the device to subdue wanted criminals.

Publicist Oxbo Lake scurried with his camera a couple of paces behind the chief, trying to find angles from which he could take candid photos of the mayoral candidate at work without revealing the disturbing decor of their location.

Campaign pictures featuring Bis Pargo standing beside a revolving wire rack display of spanking paddles and ring-gags were unlikely to present the family-man persona he wanted his client to radiate.

"What's going on here?" Pargo demanded, leaning over a distraught croupier sitting very uncomfortably on the edge of a bed of nails.

"This gentleman is giving a description of the hostage-taker to our departmental sketch artist, Chief," replied the officer, gesturing to a long-haired woman busily scraping a lump of charcoal over a sheet of paper attached to a clipboard.

"Let me see!"

The artist made a few final strokes, then handed the image to Pargo. He took the sketch over to where a single bare lightbulb hung above a large piece of dungeon equipment labeled The Rack.

"Well, well, well..." he drawled. "So this is the wannabe desperado who chose to play tough fucker on my moon, is it? Ugly bastard. Not surprising he lost his shit trying to win next week's rent on the turn of a card.

Lake peered around Pargo, eyes grew wide as he studied the sketch. "Oh, fuck!"

"What?" demanded Pargo. "What's 'oh fuck'!?"

Lake gestured to the illustration with a trembling hand,

his wide eyes flicking to the other hostages as they gave their own descriptions to other sketch artists.

"That's not just some desperado, sir!" he croaked. "That's..."

Producing his tablet, he launched the app for Taglen's most trusted news channel. "That's the escaped serial killer Vimor Malfic!"

Pargo snatched the tablet from his publicist's hands, looking from the bearded police mugshot to the artist's rendering and back again.

"No!" he breathed. "That's not him! They don't look anything alike!"

Dumping the rest of his paperwork on a stack of zoologically-themed crotchless underwear, Lake kept back one sheet of paper. Folding it in half, he drew a crude hair-free mouth and chin on it and slid the paper over the bushy beard the criminal wore in the official police photo.

The result was undeniable. The man in the sketch was Vimor Malfic.

Pargo blanched.

"Oh, fuck!"

Planet Taglen, Lymak City, Temple of Persha

"Equipment check, everyone," said Jack, sliding his modified Jean Dukes Special from its holster. He ensured the weapon was recharging correctly and that the dial which set the gun's level of power from stun to utter annihilation turned smoothly.

The team had released Dabriel Yagash twenty minutes earlier, telling him to collect his daughter Hamble from the home of the friends who cared for her during the day and go into hiding somewhere safe. Once they had Jolio Phisk in custody, he would be called upon to testify against the high priest when it came time to be tried for his crimes.

Dabriel had quickly agreed, sharing with the Shadows exactly where the bodies of self-sacrificed sinners were taken to be cut up and turned into pre-prepared packed meals made from unspecified meat—a food processing factory known simply as 'The Plant'.

At first Tc'aarlat had been uncertain whether awarding Dabriel his freedom was a wise move, but Jack had impressed upon the worried priest just how many resources the group had and how they could track him down in the event of his disappearance.

And just to be certain their prize witness wouldn't be able to vanish into thin air, he'd given Adina the nod to fix a microscopic tracking device to Dabriel's scalp while supposedly checking his head for wounds he might have sustained when he'd fainted.

Once Dabriel had set off, Jack had split the group into two teams: he and Tc'aarlat would head to the casino on Hann to apprehend High Priest Jolio Phisk, while Adina, Draven, and Callis would hurry to The Plant to retrieve Merfel Strumm's corpse before it became a main course for the planet's homeless population.

As Tc'aarlat and Adina inspected their identical weapons, Draven produced a gun that looked similar but not exactly the same.

"Ooh, I remember those!" exclaimed Adina, reaching for it. "That's the Mark Two Special. I was part of the team that worked on those, adding the upgrades suggested by agents who used them in the field."

Draven handed her his gun. "So I've got you to thank, have I?" He smiled. "This thing has saved my skin more times than I care to remember."

"All in a day's work!" Adina grinned as she held the weapon at arm's length and squinted down its line of sight.

"Well, it won't do my skin much good if you accidentally disintegrate it!" protested Tc'aarlat, dodging as Adina swung her aim from one side of the room to the other.

"Isomorphic!" Adina reminded him. "If your personal DNA signature isn't programmed into the gun's memory it won't fire." To demonstrate, she repeatedly pulled the trigger.

Until a zap of electricity caused her to squeal and drop the weapon.

Diving forward, Draven snatched the gun from the air before it could hit the ground. "I'm guessing the shock deterrent was built in to the Specials after you stopped working on them?" He smirked.

Adina sucked her tingling trigger finger and nodded.

"What about me?" asked Callis. "If I'm coming with you guys, do *I* get a gun?"

The Shadows looked at one another uneasily for a moment.

"Tell you what," said Tc'aarlat, "we'll go one better..."

The Yollin gave a shrill whistle, the signal for Mist to leave her perch on his right shoulder. She flapped across the room and perched on one of the hooks on the coat rack. As Callis watched, her feathers melted from their usual blood-red to the same green as the vestments below her.

Removing his leather shoulder pad, Tc'aarlat slid the strings over Callis' wrist and up to her armpit, where he re-tied them. Once the pad was secured on her shoulder, another whistle instructed Mist to move to her new position.

"You stay with Callis and look after her," he ordered, staring deeply into the raal hawk's eyes. "Protect her as if she were your own offspring, understand?"

SKARRRR! cried Mist, ruffling her green feathers and nuzzling her beak against Callis' ear.

"OK," said Jack. "Looks like we're set. Now, what do we know about the place where this Jolio Phisk character has gone?"

Giving her shocked hand a final shake to relieve the painful pins and needles still coursing through it, Adina pulled back the sleeve of her jacket and spoke to what appeared to be a slim silver watch strapped to her wrist.

"Solo, tell us about the Blue Diamond Casino on the Moon of Hann."

The EI's avatar appeared on the gadget's glass screen and she spoke tinnily through its speaker.

"Previously known as the Sapphire Fountain, the Blue Diamond Casino was purchased by its current owner Thavo Domp a little over a decade ago. The facility has the reputation of being able to cater to almost any personal desire, no matter how immoral, illegal, or dangerous."

Jack nodded and turned to Tc'aarlat. "You and I will take the *Pegasus* to track down Jolio Phisk. Keep your weapon at hand in case he tries anything stupid when he realizes the game's up. Draven, you, Adina, and Callis—"

"Whoa, wait a minute!" exclaimed the Yollin, holding up his hand. "Are we just going to let that go?"

Jack blinked. "Let what go?"

Tc'aarlat grabbed Adina's wrist, pushing back the sleeve of her jacket. "This!" he cried. "Since when do we have watches that allow us to talk to Solo when we're away from the ship?"

"It's not a watch!" countered Adina, pulling her arm free and angling the gizmo toward her colleague. "It's a personal communicator. It doesn't tell the time."

"Actually, I *can* tell you the time if you wish," announced Solo from Adina's wrist.

"I don't care what it's called!" barked Tc'aarlat.

"Then what's the problem?" asked Jack.

"When did we get them?!" demanded Tc'aarlat. "Have you got one?"

Jack shook his head. "It's not an official piece of *Etheric Federation* field tech," he replied. "At least, not yet. And no, I haven't got one."

"I have." Draven smiled, sliding back his shirt sleeve to reveal an identical silver device. "In fact, the one Adina's wearing is my spare."

Adina nodded. "I was able to reprogram it to work with our frequency."

Tc'aarlat closed his eyes for a second in an effort to calm himself. When he opened them again, his voice was quieter but no less firm. "If we're splitting into two teams..."

"Which we are," confirmed Jack.

"Then I don't understand why one team gets two

communicators and the other has to go without. Jack and I have got just as much need to stay in contact with Solo, if not more."

"How do you work that one out?" asked Draven.

"You lot are just scooting off to stop a dead body from being minced up and made into pies!" the Yollin declared. "Jack and I are hunting down a potentially dangerous felon."

"All right." sighed Adina, unfastening the strap on her communicator. "You can take this."

"No," Tc'aarlat insisted, pointing to Draven. "I want his."

"What?" cried Adina. "What difference does it make?"

"He said it himself!" said Tc'aarlat. "Yours is a spare. It hasn't been tested in the field. Jack and I need a device we can rely on."

"But—"

"No, buts!" declared Tc'aarlat. "We get Draven's communicator, and that's it. I'm putting my fuck down!"

"It's *foot*," Jack corrected.

"What is?"

"The thing you put down in that saying!"

"Foot?"

"Yes! You know, that thing you've shoved down your throat every time you've opened your mouth recently?"

Tc'aarlat frowned. "I don't understand."

"We've come to expect that," said Draven, handing over his wrist communicator. "Here, take it."

Tc'aarlat accepted it with a small nod. "Thank you," he said. "You may have just saved both Jack's and my life. Who knows how this degenerate priest will react when we corner him in the casino?"

"Or the hostage-taker!" added Solo from the gadget.

Everyone turned to stare at the avatar on the tiny screen.

"Say that again?" urged Jack.

"The violent serial killer who has taken hostages and barricaded himself inside the Blue Diamond Casino," replied Solo. "Didn't I mention that part?"

16

Pegasus II, **En Route to the Moon of Hann**

"Unbelievable!" exclaimed Jack as he scrolled through the local news updates on his tablet. "The two men we're after are both in the same place! What are the odds?"

Tc'aarlat shrugged. "No idea. I've never been much of a gambler."

Jack turned to look at him. "You paid for the *Fortitude* with money you scammed from a mafia poker game!"

"That wasn't gambling!" The Yollin scoffed. "That was good honest *theft*!"

He shrugged his shoulders again, then once more.

"What on Yoll are you doing?" Jack demanded, sliding his tablet away. "Don't tell me you're developing a nervous twitch."

Tc'aarlat frowned. "Something's missing."

"I could have told you that months ago," said Jack, tapping the side of his partner's head. "I think it started when you cracked your skull on that low beam in Cargo Bay Six."

"Not there!" barked Tc'aarlat, brushing Jack's hand away. "I'm talking about my shoulders. It just doesn't feel right without Mist up there. I'm used to her weight."

"Would it help if I strapped a can of soup to your collar bone?"

Tc'aarlat scowled. "You'd have to have it surgically removed from your ass first if you ever tried!" he warned.

The Yollin turned to look out of the side window. He and Jack had rushed back to the ICS _Fortitude_ and blasted off through Taglen's atmosphere toward the more fun-loving of the planet's moons.

"Solo," called Jack.

The EI's voice rang from speakers all around the plush cabin, blue LED lights pulsing in time with each syllable. "Yes, Captain?"

"Have you managed to hack in to the Hann police computers yet?"

"I'm running a cryptoanalysis program against their final layer of security as we speak, Captain. I estimate I will gain entry within the next sixty seconds."

"Thank you."

Tc'aarlat looked at Jack. "Do you think she'll be okay?"

Jack nodded, his brow furrowing. "I don't see why not. She's hacked into secure systems before and it hasn't had any adverse effect."

"Not Solo!" exclaimed Tc'aarlat. "*Mist!* Do you think she will be okay?!"

"Why shouldn't she be?"

Tc'aarlat shrugged once again, but this time his

mandibles quivered, betraying his concern. "She turned green," he said quietly. "I've only ever seen her do that once before—back when I was running guns for the Gan'barlo family. Our truck was held up by a crew from the other side of the city. We fought back, but the other driver didn't make it."

He turned to look into the darkness of space again.

"Kinlort was my friend," he continued. "We met at boarding school and just hit it off, you know? I guess because we both came from families that didn't want us. When I quit school to join the mob, he came with me. We were like brothers."

He sighed.

"Some nights I can see him lying there in the pool of his own blood as it gets bigger and bigger, Mist shrieking in my ear. We only survived because the yellow fuckers ran when they heard sirens approaching."

"I'm sorry," said Jack. "I didn't know."

Tc'aarlat shrugged again, more gently this time. "Why would you? I don't normally talk about him. Even his parents didn't want to know when I went to tell them. They wouldn't see me. I had to leave a message with their fucking butler!"

"And Mist?"

"Her feathers turned green and stayed that way for weeks," Tc'aarlat explained. "In the wild, raal hawks only ever turn that color when they're under extreme pressure, such as when their nests are attacked. But I've no idea why she'd do it now."

"Excuse me for interrupting, Captain..." Solo's voice brought an end to the conversation. "I thought you'd like to know I've broken through the police server's firewall, and I now have full access to their system."

"Find anything interesting?"

"Possibly," replied Solo. "I located the names of the hostages who have been freed from the Casino. High Priest Jolio Phisk is not among them."

"He's still inside," said Jack with a grim smile. "If we play it right, we can get both him and Malfic."

Tc'aarlat nodded his agreement. "Kill two birds with one phone."

Jack chuckled. "Exactly," he said, giving the Yollin a friendly slap on the shoulder where Mist usually sat. "Well said, my friend. Well said."

Moon of Hann, Blue Diamond Casino

Sergeant Randy Barber closed his eyes and pinched the bridge of his nose with his forefinger and thumb.

He'd felt the headache begin to build earlier that evening and had made a mental note to grab some painkillers from the first aid kit when he next stopped off at the station.

It didn't look as if that would be happening any time soon.

Now he had the early stages of a cluster headache behind his left eye. If left unchecked it would only worsen, and more likely than not evolve into a full-blown migraine.

Something he didn't want in his present situation.

He and the rest of the hostages had been ordered to sit with their backs against the bar. Malfic had told warned them the first one to do or say something he didn't like would get a bullet through the brain.

Aside from the constant chirping from the gaming machines, everything had been pretty quiet ever since.

At one point Zalah Gilt had raised his hand to request a visit to the bathroom, something Malfic had unexpectedly allowed. Taking turns, they'd each been given exactly two minutes to get to the facilities, tend to their business, and return.

If they took so much as a second longer, Malfic had promised to execute one of their fellow captives.

Almost everyone had been back within the first minute.

The felon had also permitted Nat to fetch small bottles of water from behind the bar and distribute them among the group.

Thavo Domp had asked if he could switch his water for something a little stronger and had received a black eye for his troubles.

Leaning back, Barber rested his head against the cool marbled side of the bar. Maybe if he could find a way to move away from the banks of flashing lights on the slot machines, he could—

KSSSSTTTTT!

Barber jumped as his radio hissed into life.

"Sergeant Barber, this is Chief Bis Pargo," the cheap speaker squawked. "Are you receiving me, over?"

"Give me that!" thundered a voice.

Barber looked up to find the imposing of figure Vimor Malfic towering over him, hand outstretched.

Blinking hard in an attempt to reduce the pain behind

his eyes, he unclipped the radio from his belt and handed it over.

"Sergeant Barber!" spat Pargo again. "Are you receiving me, over?"

Malfic pressed the 'talk' button on his side of the device and growled into the microphone.

"Sergeant Barber can't come to the phone right now," he rumbled. "You can talk to me."

There was a slight pause, during which each of the remaining hostages turned to stare up at their captor as he began to pace back and forth.

When Pargo spoke again his voice had changed. Gone was the sharp, angry tone he had used before. Instead, he now sounded quieter and less certain of himself.

He sounded scared.

"M-Mr. Malfic, this is Police Chief Pis Bargo, er... I mean, Bis Pargo."

"I know who you are," Malfic snarled. "And I know *where* you are."

"Y-you do?"

Malfic glared through the casino's glass doors. In reality, all he could see were the flashing blue lights of the assembled police cars and little else, but he knew there were likely to be a couple of cameras out there as well, each providing a live video feed to the Chief wherever he was hiding. They would also be recording the entire siege for future tacticians to study, working out how they could operate differently the next time some bastard found himself in a similar position.

Vimor Malfic, serial killer and case study for training purposes.

The radio hissed with static again and Pargo spoke again. "Now that we've introduced ourselves, why don't you tell me what you want?"

Malfic paused to think about this for a moment. What *did* he want?

Before everything had gone tits-up his only plan had been to change his clothes, buy a stolen ship, and get the fuck off this rotting bistok bollock of a moon.

He hadn't even been sure where he would go.

One of the five planets in the Ordanian Hub seemed to be the best bet. There, the worlds were ruled by criminals and gangs of every persuasion.

Skolar Major and Talth were home to the most violent crime families the galaxy had ever seen, Skolar Minor was a haven for drug smugglers, and the residents of Beema trafficked in people for any number of despicable uses. Finally, the smallest world, Chakk, was in many ways similar to the Moon of Hann. It was where the criminals from the other worlds socialized, made deals, settled scores and engaged in any number of illegal pastimes.

As far as Malfic was concerned, it didn't matter which of these five infamous planets he made his home. He'd be with his own kind once again.

But first he'd need some form of transport.

"You want these hostages alive?" he demanded into the radio.

"Ideally, yes," replied Pargo. "That is, if you don't mind."

At the bar, Sergeant Barber lowered his head and blew out his cheeks. Where the hell was the unit's negotiator?

"Then I want a ship!" snarled Malfic. "Something able to

get me out of this system, and no twatting tracking devices! Got it?"

"No...twatting...devices..." repeated Pargo, obviously writing down the hostage-taker's demands. "Anything else?"

"Yeah!" cried Thavo Domp. "I'm starving over here! We need food!"

The rest of the hostages muttered their agreement, although not quite as forcefully as Domp.

Malfic sneered at them. "Food?!"

Domp nodded. "I'd kill for a pizza."

Planet Taglen, Lymak City, Temple of Persha

"Blessed is the Goddess Persha."

Adina pressed the red button on the communicator's handset to end the call and turned to Draven and Callis. "We're on."

"It worked?" asked the teenager.

Adina nodded. "They believed I'm a warden, that we had a member of our congregation turn up unexpectedly to confess to being a sinner, and that he self-sacrificed by way of penance."

"And they're coming for his body?" inquired Draven.

"They said they'd be here in around twenty minutes," replied Adina. "We'd better get you ready."

She took the golden box down from its shelf and lifted the lid. Inside on its velvet pillow sat the Dagger of Persha. Its blade was still smeared with blood from its last victim, Merfel Strumm.

"Are you sure you want to go through with this?"

"We don't have another option if we want to find this mysterious Plant where sinners' bodies are taken," Draven replied. "It'll hurt for a while afterwards, but like all *Wechselbalg* I heal quickly."

Callis frowned. "Wechselbalg?"

Draven raised his hands, fingers bent like claws. "I'm a werewolf!"

"Oh, you mean like—"

A sharp look from Adina cut off her sentence.

Draven tilted his head slightly. "Like?"

"Like...in old stories?" Callis finished, much to Adina's relief.

"Sort of," said Draven. "Only without all the howling at the moon. Now, we'd better find one of those cheap caskets Dabriel told us about."

"Won't they spot that you're still breathing?" the teenager asked.

"It's possible," said Draven. "But luckily I've got these with me..."

He produced a small bottle of pills and gave them a shake.

"What are they?"

"The eggheads at the forensic pharmacy on the *Meredith Reynolds* created them for field operatives to use in times of emergency. They'll drastically slow my heart rate and respiratory system, putting me into a kind of hibernation. Unless the staff at The Plant examine me with a stethoscope I'll appear to be utterly dead."

"Isn't that dangerous?"

"Possibly," said Draven, "but I have it on good authority from the guys in the lab that so long as I take the antidote within two hours I'll be absolutely fine. Now, let's find me somewhere to sleep."

They found a storeroom filled with flimsy wooden coffins ten minutes later. Inside the room were boxes of several different sizes, from full-length adult caskets through smaller models for children, right down to tiny boxes that could only be there to hold infants.

"How can they possibly be classed as sinners?" demanded Adina through clenched teeth. "I can't wait to get my hands on this ass-badger Phisk!"

Choosing one of the longer boxes, they dragged it out into the central aisle of the temple. Draven lifted his leg to climb inside.

Adina grabbed his arm. "Aren't you forgetting something?"

Draven's eyes narrowed as he ran through their plan in his head. "No, I don't think so."

"You're supposed to be a sinner," Adina reminded him.

Draven beamed. "Really? You're going to make me commit a sin?"

"Only if you want to do this properly..."

"OK," laughed Draven. "So, which sin would you like me to choose?"

"Corlon Strumm said his wife had blasphemed," Callis pointed out.

Draven shrugged. "OK," he said, clearing his throat. "Here goes..."

Tossing his head back, Draven stared up toward the vaulted ceiling of the vast temple. "Oi, Bitch-tits!"

Callis snorted a noisy laugh. Adina shushed her, but she was giggling too.

"Yeah, I'm talking to you Persha, you slack-minged rat-reamer! Why don't you take your three precious laws and stick 'em right up your love-trumpet, you floppy-knock-ered dick-faced piss-gargler! You've got a face like a smashed pie and you smell like a dead hobo's ballsack!"

There were a few seconds of silence after Draven's words echoed and died, and for a brief moment the trio half-expected to be struck down by bolts of lightning from the heavens.

But that didn't happen.

Draven spun on the spot and took a deep, theatrical bow as Adina and Callis both clapped and cheered.

"Reckon that will do?" he asked, climbing into the coffin and settling into position. He took a moment to shake out a pill and dry-swallow it.

"Well, I can't see her putting any of that in her next lonely-hearts ad." Adina chuckled. "I think we're good to go."

Laying his arms by his sides, Draven took a deep breath and smiled up at his new friend. "Whenever you're ready."

Callis set the box down on a nearby bench and glanced over her shoulder. "Guys, I can hear a truck pulling up outside."

"Are you sure?"

Draven lifted his arm and took Adina's hand in his, giving it a gentle squeeze. "I trust you completely."

Nodding, Adina reached inside the ornate golden box for the Dagger of Persha. Then she raised it high above her head, steeled her nerves, and plunged the glinting blade into Draven's chest

17

Moon of Hann, Deserted Parking Lot

The *Pegasus II* landed smoothly in the deserted parking lot and the doors swung open to allow Jack and Tc'aarlat to climb out.

While the lot's only lighting was a single buzzing bulb set high atop a rusting metal pole, the surrounding streets emitted a sheen of light that rendered nearby stars almost impossible to see in the night sky.

Tc'aarlat frowned as a cacophony of sounds assaulted his ears. Pounding music from night clubs, the cries of street vendors hawking their wares, and drunken shouts of gangs of roving party-goers combined to create a hubbub of jarring noises that set his teeth on edge.

Jack noticed his sour expression and smiled. "And you say I never take you anywhere nice!"

Tc'aarlat's mandibles quivered. "What a shithole!" he spat. "Totally reminds me of home."

TOM DUBLIN & MICHAEL ANDERLE

Jack's eyebrows shot up. "*This* reminds you of Yoll?"

Tc'aarlat nodded. "Despicable people with more money than sense wallowing in pure pleasure at the expense of those around them? My parents could well be sponsoring this place."

Chuckling, Jack tapped his personal access code into the number pad on the secure weapons storage area at the rear of the shuttle. The glossy black cover slid back with a hiss.

Inside, packed in specially-cut foam, was an assortment of weapons ranging from old-style projectile guns to huge anti-personnel-carrier blasters.

Tc'aarlat whistled. "Nice! And here was me thinking we'd just need our Jean Dukes Specials."

Jack snatched a pair of folding knives, handing one to the Yollin and tucking the other in his pocket. "That's what I'm hoping, but it doesn't hurt to have a little something in reserve."

Closing the locker, Jack returned to the side door of the ship. "Solo," he said, leaning into the passenger area, "keep a close eye on the police comm channel. Let us know if the situation at the casino changes in any way."

"Certainly, Captain," the EI replied. "May I be so bold as to ask what you and Tc'aarlat are planning to do?"

"Simple, really," Jack replied, winking at Tc'aarlat. "We're going to fuck up some bad guys."

Planet Taglen, Lymak City, Highway 19

Adina shifted the vehicle into fifth gear and stomped on

the gas pedal in an effort to keep up with the truck containing Draven's casket.

While the vehicle she'd borrowed from Dabriel might have been a perfectly efficient way to get around in day-to-day city traffic, it lacked the power required to come anywhere close to the speed limit of the highways leading out of town.

Coupled with its flimsy frame and cramped interior, this was like chasing a eighteen-wheeler in a golf cart.

Due to the numerous religious artifacts Dabriel had mounted inside the vehicle, Adina had taken to calling it "The Pershamobile."

"There!" cried Callis, pointing to the heavy evening traffic ahead of them. "There's the truck!"

Adina squinted through the thick windshield, which felt as if it were made of transparent plastic rather than glass. The combination of the rear lights of other vehicles and the approaching dusk made keeping their target in sight difficult.

Dabriel had insisted he didn't know the location of The Plant, so Adina knew if they lost sight of the transport they wouldn't know where Draven was being taken.

"They're turning off!" said Callis.

"I see them!" confirmed Adina. She fumbled through an array of unmarked switches on the dash, looking for the one that would turn on her indicator. She found the right control on the third try, after first turning on the rear wiper and making both of them jump as some kind of kindergarten hip-hop song blasted from the speakers.

Once they were off the highway it became easier to

follow the truck. Although no one seemed to know the actual address of The Plant, the fact that it had taken approximately twenty minutes after Adina's call for the collection van to arrive gave her hope that it wasn't too far away.

Adina kept eyeing the charge indicator warily as it crept closer and closer to empty.

"They're turning again," said Callis as the truck slowed and illuminated its right blinker.

Adina held back, switching off their headlights—first try!—and waiting until their prey had disappeared around the corner before moving on. The last thing she wanted was for the two men driving the vehicle to spot them in their rearview mirror.

Two turns later a vast gray factory loomed into view. Adina and Callis pulled over and watched as the truck backed up to a loading bay and the driver killed the engine.

The vehicle's doors swung open and the two men who had collected the casket from the temple jumped out.

Although pretending to be a warden on the phone had gone smoothly, Adina wasn't certain that imitating one in person would be quite as easy. She had taken the white robe from the guard at the main door and slipped it over her clothes, keeping her gun within easy reach in case her cover was blown.

Shortly after she'd let the two guys from The Plant inside the older of the pair had asked after Sedrin, the warden they had expected to be met by. Adina had given the excuse that he was out sick and not, in reality, tied up in a storage closet less than thirty feet away with Callis standing over him wielding a long silver candlestick to ensure he stayed quiet.

They had, however, ensured he wouldn't be trapped inside the closet for much longer; Adina had left a note on the altar informing the next wardens to turn up for duty exactly where to find their constrained colleague.

Thankfully the ruse had worked. The two men had glanced at Draven, muttered a prayer to the goddess, then stepped back to allow Adina to pull the Dagger of Persha from his chest and return it to its ceremonial box.

As the collectors were fixing the casket's lid in place she caught sight of fresh blood flowing from Draven's wound and staining his shirt—a clear indication that he was still alive and his body was starting to heal itself.

She quickly engaged the two men in an inane conversation about the weather to keep their attention as they worked. By the time they were ready to leave, they both seemed glad to get away from this crazed, chatty stand-in for their friend.

After the men went inside, Adina and Callis climbed out of Dabriel's car and made their way on foot toward the imposing building.

It was at least half the size of the temple, although nowhere near as ornate or decorative. In fact, if they hadn't followed the truck they would have no way of knowing it was a factory to turn fresh corpses into food.

Only a handful of windows were lit, mainly on the second and third floors. Practically everything at ground level was dark, indicating as Dabriel had suggested that the majority of The Plant's workers had gone home for the day.

Suddenly the side door swung open again, sending a shaft of light out over the loading bay and just catching Adina's foot as she and Callis hid behind a stack of damaged caskets.

There was a low clattering *whirrr* as the mechanical shutters sealing the interior loading area rolled up. Thankfully the collectors didn't turn on any lights inside, leaving plenty of darkness to help conceal the two women as they watched the men work.

Peering through gaps in the pile of coffins, the pair looked on as the men unlocked the rear of their truck and made three trips to carry the same number of caskets inside.

One of the collectors went around the back of the truck to close and lock the doors while the other hit the button to close the loading bay shutters, which slowly began to rumble back down.

This was it: the only real opportunity Callis and Adina would have to get inside, at least without drawing attention to themselves.

As soon as the collectors turned to head back in through the side door, Adina gestured silently to her colleague and the two women raced across the parking lot toward the loading bay.

Ahead of them, the rolled metal shutters continued to clatter downwards, quickly sealing off their only hope of saving Draven and finding Merfel's body without resorting to violence.

They reached the dock just as the shutters approached the ground. Adina dived for the gap, rolling underneath the metal screen as it sank lower and lower.

A second later Callis made the same move but hit her elbow on the bottom of the shutter with a resounding *thud* as it dropped. Adina quickly reached out to grab Callis by the arm and drag her in across the dusty concrete floor.

There was a metallic *clunk* as the shutter made contact with the concrete and the two women froze, listening hard in case Callis' collision had alerted any of the staff.

For almost a minute neither of them dared to move, and it was almost thirty more seconds before Adina realized she was holding her breath. She let out a silent gasp and worked to restore her breathing to its normal rate.

It soon became clear that no one had heard the noise, or if they had they weren't coming to investigate. Adina helped Callis to her feet, then whispered into her wrist communicator.

"Solo, can you throw a little light on the situation, please?"

Without replying, the EI lit up the circular screen of the device, essentially providing Adina with a wrist-mounted flashlight. She swept the beam from one side of the room to the other, showing them where they were and what they were dealing with.

Callis gasped. They were inside some kind of warehouse filled with row after row of tall shelving units.

Each shelf was filled with identical plain wooden caskets.

"Where do we start?" she hissed.

"I *would* suggest we split up," whispered Adina in reply, "but we only have one flashlight. I guess we just begin at one end and work our way to the other.

Callis followed Adina to the first row of floor-to-ceiling

shelves and watched as she tapped each casket in turn on the lowest shelf.

There was only silence.

As she worked her way higher and higher, knocking on each of the coffins as she went, she felt Callis gently tug at her sleeve.

"What is it?" she asked.

"Your ears!" replied the teenager quietly, pointing to the top of Adina's head. "Can't you do your wolf-ears trick again and listen for his heartbeat or something?"

Adina was torn. She knew that Callis' idea would most likely help them locate Draven far more quickly, but she risked him spotting her partial transformation before she could return her ears to their human form.

She still didn't want to give away the fact that she was a werewolf just like him.

That said, time was running out. Thanks to the heavy traffic, the trip to The Plant had taken much longer than expected. Adina now had less than thirty minutes to give Draven the antidote to the pill he had taken to appear deceased, or any damage to his internal organs could become permanent.

And tapping on each of the hundreds of caskets in this huge facility was going to take a lot longer than that.

She sighed and nodded. Taking a couple of steps back from Callis, Adina gritted her teeth and for the second time that day concentrated on overriding the DNA-dampening medication she took daily to prevent her from changing into a werewolf.

A few moments later a pair of tall, furry wolf ears were twitching on top of her skull.

A smile spread across her still-firmly-human face.

"Got him!"

Turning her wrist to aim the beam of light from her comm at the floor, she hurried across the warehouse to the third stack from the end. Then, stepping slowly and quietly, she zeroed in on the only coffin with a still-beating heart inside.

With Callis' help she lifted the casket off the shelf and laid it on the ground, then Adina quietly commanded Solo to switch off the light and disappeared into the darkness.

Using a multitool Jack had given her, Callis worked quickly to remove the screws holding the box's lid in place. It wasn't easy working in the near darkness, but she found she could locate the screws by running her fingertips along the outer edges of the lid.

After a short while, Callis removed the final fastener and, tucking the multitool away, she grabbed both sides of the lid and lifted it off.

Inside, barely breathing was Draven, his shirt now almost completely soaked with blood from the knife wound in his chest. Callis swallowed hard. Had they underestimated how much he would lose while being transported here?

Fishing the bottle of antidote capsules from her pocket, she held Draven's mouth open and crushed one of the pills into it with her fingers.

Callis snapped the cap back on and returned the bottle to her pocket, crossing the fingers on her other hand. Then she waited.

Nothing happened.

Callis pressed her hand to Draven's bloody chest,

searching for his heartbeat. It was there, but very slow and dangerously weak.

She pulled the bottle of pills back out of her pocket, her own heart beginning to pound. Had she given him the right medication at the right time? Callis was certain he'd told her he only needed one of them to counteract the effects of the stuff he'd taken to slow down his system, but it didn't seem to be working. Could she risk giving him another dose without endangering his life?

"Come on, Draven," she hissed. "Come back to us! You can do it!"

Callis tightened her grip on the pill bottle, her thumb pressing hard against the edge of the lid. If nothing happened within the next minute she would break open another capsule and—

Suddenly Draven's eyes shot wide open and he gasped in a huge lungful of air.

The antidote had worked!

As Callis helped him to sit up and regulate his breathing, Adina stepped out of the shadows to kneel beside the casket.

To her obvious relief, she looked completely human once more.

"How are you?" she asked, brushing Draven's tousled hair from his eyes.

"Did I do it right?" questioned Callis, concern etched on her features.

"I'm not sure," croaked Draven, his eyes flickering from one of his rescuers to the other. "Something feels strange..."

The two women' eyes met in dismay.

"Why?" demanded Adina. "What's wrong?"

Draven's face split into a wide grin. "Because I've woken up to find myself faced with a pair of angels! I think I may have died for real!"

The hard slap Adina landed across his left cheek echoed painfully around the warehouse.

Moon of Hann, Outside The Blue Diamond Casino

Miles of yellow Do Not Cross tape fluttered in the warm evening breeze, lit by the flashing blue lights of what might have been every single police car in the entire Hann department.

Jack and Tc'aarlat eased their way through the crowds of rubbernecking aliens, ducked under the tape, and made for the group of uniformed officers camped out on the opposite side of the street from the casino.

"Him!" said Tc'aarlat, pointing to a stout figure clutching a megaphone. His dark-blue shirt bulged at the stomach to the point of giving the appearance of late-term pregnancy. "He's in charge!"

As the pair approached, several of the officers on the outer edge of the group turned to block their progress.

Jack pulled out his wallet and flipped it open to reveal an all-too-brief glimpse of a photo ID card as the pair approached. "Jack Marber, official *Etheric Federation* envoy," he announced. "This is my colleague Tc'aarlat. We'd like to talk to your boss."

The assembled cops glanced at one another, uncertain how to best respond to the new arrivals.

"I said *now*, officers!" barked Jack, causing one of the cops to scuttle in the direction of the chief.

Tc'aarlat turned to Jack as they waited. "When did you get an *Etheric Federation* ID?" he asked quietly.

"I didn't," replied Jack conspiratorially as he tucked his wallet away. "That was my library card."

The messenger barked an order and the wall of cops parted, allowing the pair access to the inner circle of command.

Tc'aarlat gave each of the lower-ranked officers a stern glare as he passed just to keep their nerves on edge.

Bis Pargo raised the megaphone to his mouth as the two men approached. From just behind him a slimmer figure with bleached-blond facial hair hissed, "Other hand, sir!"

With a grunt, the police chief dropped the megaphone and replaced it with the radio in his other hand.

"This is Chief Pargo," he spat into the handset. "Operation Deep Pan is go. I repeat, Operation Deep Pan is go!"

"Excuse me," began Jack. "We are representatives of the—"

"I don't care who the fuck you represent, son," Pargo interrupted. "You will remain silent while you watch me put an end to this entire fiasco."

Tc'aarlat's mandibles quivered. "What did you—"

Jack raised a hand to cut him off.

"Let's see how this plays out."

The sound of a revving engine caught their attention. Across the street, a pizza delivery guy on a moped drew up outside the closed casino doors and dropped the kickstand.

Darting to the crate fixed to the rear of the bike, he removed a stack of pizza boxes and, readjusting his cap, approached the entrance to the building.

When he was outside the doors, they swung open to reveal the bikini-clad greeter, Deedee Joh, and the croupier, Nat Farrow. There was movement in the shadows somewhere behind the women, but neither Jack nor Tc'aarlat could work out who—or what—was there.

"He's too confident," hissed Jack to his colleague.

"Meaning what?" Tc'aarlat whispered back.

"He's not from the pizza place," replied Jack. "If he was, he'd look more nervous."

"You think he's a—"

Before Tc'aarlat could finish his question the delivery boy sprang into action. As the two females reached out to accept the stack of boxes, the deliverer dumped them all to the ground, except for the one at the bottom of the pile.

This box he tore open, reaching inside to grab the handle of a gun hidden under the surface of the pie. The delivery guy tried to drag it free from the layer of cheese covering it, but the weapon became stuck as he pulled, lifting the entire pizza out of the box with it.

Before he could rid the barrel of pepperoni a shot rang out, making both Nat and Deedee jump and run for cover inside.

The pizza delivery boy spun on the spot, awarding the entire task force a brief glimpse of the flowering red hole in his throat before he fell to the pavement, dead.

"Fucking idiots!" growled Tc'aarlat as Bis Pargo's advisors crowded around him.

Across the street, the casino doors slammed shut as Pargo's radio hissed into life.

"You really think I'm that stupid, fuckball?!" roared Malfic. "Just for that, I'm going to send *you* a special delivery! One of the hostages is about to get a bullet in the brain and it's all down to you, shit-for-brains!"

Jack pushed his way through the officers to get to Pargo, Tc'aarlat at his heels. "Let us sort this out," he urged. "We have a vested interest in getting both Malfic and one of his hostages out of there. We need them both alive!"

Chief Pargo glared at the pair for a moment, then turned to his second-in-command. "Get these two clowns out of here!" he bellowed. "*Now!*"

As a stern-faced cop shoved Jack and Tc'aarlat back under the nearest strip of police tape, the Yollin clenched his fists.

"So, what now? We have to do something before that asswipe gets everyone in there killed."

"Well," suggested Jack as they marched away from the crime scene. "We just have to find another way inside."

Moon of Hann, Inside The Blue Diamond Casino

"Get up there, all of you!"

Vimor Malfic's face flushed a deep purple as he pushed each of the hostages onto the staircase leading up to Thavo Domp's office with the barrel of his weapon.

How dare those bastards try to trick him like that?!

Fuckers! It was time to send them a message to show exactly how serious he was.

Zalah Gilt reached the door at the top of the narrow staircase and stopped. "It's locked!" he called back down.

"Who has the keys?" demanded Malfic.

"I do!" replied Domp, second from the end. He fished a ring of keys attached to a shimmering blue gemstone from his trouser pocket and jingled them in Malfic's direction."

"Then get up there!"

"Yes," grumbled Domp, clearly not used to being ordered around his own casino. "Of course."

The others pressed themselves against the wall to leave room for Domp to squeeze past them, but due to the narrowness of the stair case and the width of the casino owner this wasn't an easy process.

Eventually Domp had to press his expansive stomach hard against the wooden handrail, sliding the blubbery mass along it as he climbed past his fellow captives.

Reaching the top, he nudged Gilt aside and unlocked his office with trembling fingers.

Finally the door swung open.

"Inside!" roared Malfic.

The group filed into the office, unsure what they were supposed to do next. Once Malfic was inside, he slammed the door and held out his hand toward Domp for the keys.

The casino owner began to work at getting his blue diamond keyring off the loop, but Malfic obviously didn't have the patience to watch him fiddle with the clasp.

"Now!"

Sighing, Domp reluctantly handed over the entire ring, gemstone and all. Malfic passed his gun to his left hand,

and kept it aimed at the group while he worked with the other to determine which was the office key.

Once everyone was locked inside, he switched the weapon back to his right hand.

"Sit!" he commanded, twitching the barrel of his gun toward the leather sofa running along one wall of the room. Sergeant Barber gestured for Nat and Deedee to sit first, scowling as Jolio Phisk and Thavo Domp helped themselves to the remaining seats without a word.

Not wanting to cause any further problems, he simply nodded to Zalah Gilt and both men lowered themselves to the carpet in front of a glass display case containing a collection of golden poker chips.

"Wh-what are you going to do?" asked Deedee Joh as Malfic paced up and down the small room.

"Quiet!" Malfic snarled, spinning on the hostages. He wiped his hand across his face. "Those bastards! Those sphincter-ripping shit-sucking bastards! I'm gonna send them a message they'll never forget!"

"Calm down," urged Jolio Phisk. "Remember what the Goddess Persha taught us about tranquility. She—"

Click!

Malfic cocked his gun, raised the weapon in the air, and slowly lowered it to point directly at Phisk's pallid face.

"A message they'll *never* fucking forget."

Staring down the black interior of the barrel, Phisk screwed his eyes shut. An icy chill coursed down his spine.

Then came the *BOOM*! Deafening within the confines of the tiny office. Several of the hostages jumped and cried out...and the poker chips inside the glass case clattered as they fell from their carefully positioned display.

For a few seconds Phisk's senses were at war. His ears rang, his skin prickled, he tasted bile in his throat, and his nostrils burned with the fumes from Malfic's gun.

That only left his sight.

After sending the command for his eyes to open Phisk turned his head to left, which brought Thavo Domp into view.

Or more specifically, the smoking red crater in the center of the casino owner's forehead.

Planet Taglen, Lymak City, The Plant

"Twelve," hissed Adina as she lowered her communicator and reviewed the snippet of video Solo had recorded through the dust-coated window of the control room's door. "We've got twelve individuals inside."

"Why so many?" questioned Callis.

Adina shrugged. "I guess in case they're called out to collect corpses elsewhere in the city," she theorized. "The temple isn't the only place to worship Persha in and around Lymak. Dabriel said there were a number of smaller churches dotted about the suburbs."

"And they'll need a core team to stay behind and watch over this place," added Draven. He glanced back over the immense warehouse. "Although I doubt this lot are likely to rise up and rebel against their jailers anytime soon."

The trio had searched the racks of coffins for the one containing the remains of Merfel Strumm, but as Adina had pointed out it was like looking for a needle in a huge stack of identical needles.

Each of the caskets was labeled, but only with a code

comprised of letters and numbers—not with the incumbent's name. It could take them days to stumble across the right box if they were to simply pry off each individual lid and peer inside.

Doing so had rewarded Draven with a shirt to replace the one soaked with his blood, though. The stab wound on his chest was still healing and he knew he was likely to experience discomfort for some time to come, but the only real harm was the loss of one of his favorite wardrobe items.

"Trust me to wear an expensive shirt on the day I volunteer myself as a knife victim," he commented as he stripped the top from a corpse of a similar size and build to his own.

"Thanks, fella!" He patted the dead man on the shoulder and stuffed his bloodied garment into the casket beside him, then replaced the lid.

"I don't like it," said Adina.

"What?" questioned Draven. "Is it the color? I can't really tell in the dark, but I reckon I've always suited teal."

"Not the shirt!" retorted Adina. "This whole set-up. Taking the bodies of the dead and grinding them up as food for other people."

The group had found the doors leading to the processing area of The Plant but had decided not to explore that particular wing of the facility. Other departments listed on a site map affixed to the wall beside the entrance had included Kitchen, Packing, and Tasting.

"This place gives me the creeps," Adina had said with a shudder.

"Nothing a handful of carefully-placed high-explosives

wouldn't solve," Draven had pointed out. "I know this lot are already past the living and breathing stage of their existence, but this entire concept proves there are indeed things worse than death."

They continued exploring the building, searching for some sort of filing system or even a computer terminal so they could locate Merfel Strumm.

"Did everyone here self-sacrifice?" asked Callis. "If so, there's an awful lot of sinning going on."

"According to what Dabriel said, anyone who dies from anything other than a natural death ends up here," related Adina. "Even being the victim of murder is considered contrary to the laws of their precious goddess."

"I hope Jack and Tc'aarlat are able to get their hands on that high priest guy," said Draven. "I wouldn't mind having a brief one-on-one chat with him in a locked room."

Eventually they came across a doorway with light streaming out through a small circular window near the top. They heard several voices inside, and by removing her communicator Adina was able to record the scene. The room appeared to double as an office for those collectors assigned the overnight shift and, judging by the banks of computers and multiple screens along the far wall, a central control room.

Adina slipped the communicator back onto her wrist. "We need a way to neutralize all twelve of them."

"I could invite my wolf to the party," suggested Draven.

"No!" Adina insisted. "We need a non-lethal strategy. If we kill them we become as bad as them. I'm not doing it that way."

"I wasn't suggesting he kill them," explained Draven.

"We just use him to scare them a little; keep them occupied while you two get in there and search the system."

Adina's eyebrows raised. "You can restrain your wolf like that? It would just hold them back without attacking?"

"Absolutely," promised Draven. "And my wolf is a 'he,' not an 'it.'"

"Okay, what would *he* do if those goons decided their best course of action was to team up and attack him? What then?"

Draven frowned. "He wouldn't do anything. I can control him."

"Completely?"

"Completely!"

Adina shook her head. "I can't risk it. If you lose your temper—"

"It wouldn't happen."

"I don't believe that."

"Why?"

"I... I just don't!"

The pair fell into an awkward silence, the argument having reached an uneasy stalemate.

Callis raised a finger as an idea occurred to her. "They can't attack the wolf if they're unconscious..."

19

Planet Taglen, Lymak City, The Plant, Control Room

Garr Kilb slapped a spread of four cards down on the table and grinned. "Read 'em and weep, sucker!" He laughed, leaning back in his chair and taking a sip from his bottle of soda.

Rog Rye peered at his colleague's cards, lips moving as he did the mental arithmetic required to work out just how much he had lost. "Twenty-eight exactly!" he groaned. "How the fuck did you manage that?"

"A little thing called skill!" responded Kilb, holding out his hand and rubbing his thumb across his fingertips. "Pay up."

"Skill, my ass!" grumbled Rye, digging into his pocket and counting out a number of copper coins, each worth a hundredth of a credit. "You're cheating somehow. I don't know how, but you're definitely cheating!"

The two friends had been playing Make Twenty-Eight for the equivalent of pennies five nights a week for several years now. Over time the amount each man won or lost had remained roughly the same, but Kilb's recent rash of winning hands was beginning to make his pal suspicious.

All around the room, the night-shift collectors passed the time in their usual ways between pick-ups. Mart Pell read horror novels, Stev Hender quietly twiddled away at a stringed instrument, and Aln Borl connected digital bubbles into rows of three or more in order to pop them and win points by saving trapped animals on his tablet.

The night was passing exactly as so many others had done before. Until, that is, the door swung open and a teenager with some kind of green bird perched on her shoulder stepped into the room.

"Excuse me," she began, smiling. "Does anyone have the correct time?"

SKAWWWWWW!

Each of the twelve men stopped what they were doing and stared. Rog Rye dropped his coins. Mart Pell lost his place in his book. And Aln Borl's tablet played a brief consolatory tune to accompany the 'Game Over' text spinning in the center of the screen.

The young female turned and ran out of the room, disappearing into the darkness of the warehouse beyond. For a split-second no one on the night shift moved, then they all leaped to their feet as one and gave chase.

Excluding the brief but comical moment when they all attempted to squeeze through the doorway at the same time, the speed at which they pursued the trespasser would most likely have pleased their superiors.

But that was nothing compared to how quickly they

came to a halt when the large wolf stepped out of the shadows and snarled.

The creature was covered with sleek golden fur, its eyes were a fierce bright yellow, and its razor-sharp teeth glinted almost as much as its equally lethal claws in the shaft of light escaping from the control room behind them.

This standoff continued for a few seconds, broken only when Rog Rye reached out to snatch up a heavy crowbar from the nearest shelf and took a hesitant step forward.

A burst of blue light exploded in the blackness behind the wolf, briefly lighting up the face of a second female—this one clutching a gun in both hands—before streaking across the short distance between the two sides and striking Rog Rye in the chest.

Crying out, the collector collapsed to the ground. He was out cold.

Then the chaos began.

Together, the remaining eleven members of The Plant's night shift charged at the wolf and the woman, their faces twisted in expressions of rage.

The gun spat blast after blast of blue light, taking down whichever of the men happened to be at the forefront of the group at that particular moment.

Aln Borl spotted movement in the shadows to his right from the corner of his eye and turned to find the teenage girl watching the attack play out.

Breaking off from the group, he ran toward her with his arms outstretched, ready to grab her throat and squeeze until she dropped to the floor as unconscious as his fallen colleagues.

He didn't get that far.

As he neared her the green bird sitting on her shoulder took flight. Spreading its wings wide, the hawk soared through the air, outstretched claws almost mimicking the way Borl held his hands.

Before the collector had time to reconsider his attack the bird's talons dug deep into the skin of his face, ripping and tearing at his flesh. Borl screamed as the hawk began to stab at his wide, terrified eyes with its sharp curved beak.

There was a noise like air being sucked out of a balloon and a blast of blue collided with Borl's chest, throwing him backward and mercifully sending every last drop of consciousness running for safety.

The final collector hit the concrete as he wrestled with the wolf, his hands pressed to the sides of the animal's head, elbows locked, as he fought to keep the powerful snapping jaws as far away as possible.

As the echoes of the attack died away, the werewolf padded over to where Adina was standing.

She took a step away.

Draven trotted away into the darkness of the casket stacks.

By the time he returned, now looking decidedly human and once again fully dressed, Adina and Callis had tied up ten of the dozen men.

"They won't come around for at least another hour," Adina informed them. "We'll be long gone by then."

Nodding, Draven strode past the women toward a computer terminal in the control room. It took him a couple of minutes to familiarize himself with the operating system, but before long he had gained access to the data-base of current occupants.

"Merfel Strumm, stack ten, shelf eleven," he read aloud. He pushed back his chair and stood, then paused to pick up a discarded book. He checked the cover and read the blurb on the back, then set the novel aside and left the room to rejoin his teammates.

Thirty minutes later he, Adina, and Callis had finished loading the unconscious men into the back of one of the facility's trucks and parked it a half-mile down the access road that led to The Plant.

Switching vehicles, they stowed Merfel's casket on the back seat and they took off.

Shortly afterwards a large enough cloud of gas had escaped from the pipeline they had severed to reach the playing cards and broken pieces of string instrument they had left burning in the control room's wastepaper basket.

The trio did not look back at the explosion that destroyed The Plant.

Moon of Hann, The Blue Diamond Casino, Rear Loading Bay

Tc'aarlat finished unscrewing the metal grille covering the vent for the casino's air conditioning system and climbed off the stack of abandoned beer crates he had used to reach it.

"After you," he said, tossing the grille aside. It clattered as it hit the ground.

"Are you *trying* to attract attention?" Jack demanded,

climbing onto the crates and lifting himself into the metal duct beyond. "Because if you are, you're doing a great job."

"Thanks!" proclaimed Tc'aarlat, missing Jack's sarcastic tone as he climbed into the duct behind his friend. "I'll admit I consider myself to be biumphant when blending in."

Jack crawled forward a few feet, then paused. "What?" he queried over his shoulder. "What the fuck is 'biumphant' supposed to mean?!"

"It's like 'triumphant', but not quite as good," explained the Yollin.

Jack continued crawling deeper into the system. "Run that one by me again..."

Tc'aarlat sighed, his mandibles tapping together as he followed. "You humans have the word 'triumphant,' right?"

"Right."

"A word which means you've won or been successful at something."

"Yes..."

"But if you don't quite achieve that level, the *tri*umphant level, you'd be one step down from there. Logically that would be *bi*umphant."

Jack blinked as he crawled. "My brain hurts."

"Hey, don't blame me," insisted Tc'aarlat. "This is one of your weird human expressions we're talking about."

Jack reached a junction and opted to take the left-hand tunnel.

"How is it weird?!" he asked.

"Well," said Tc'aarlat, "tricycles have three wheels and tripods have three legs, right?"

"I guess."

Tc'aarlat's mandibles spread wide. "Following that logic, 'triumphant' must mean the word has three 'umphs'."

"What the fuck is an 'umph?'"

"How the hell should I know?"

"OK, whatever," said Jack. "But, I do know the 'tri' part of triumphant doesn't refer to the number three."

"Then what does it mean?"

Jack thought for a second, but that only confused him further. "I... I've no idea," he admitted at last.

"So, it *might* mean three."

"Three umphs?"

"Exactly!"

"I suppose. But then, why have three of them?"

"Who knows?" replied Tc'aarlat. "Maybe an 'umph' is a cheer?"

"A cheer?" mused Jack. "How'd you work that one out?"

"Three cheers!" responded the Yollin. "If they're triumphant at whatever it is they've set out to achieve, humans often give three cheers."

"True."

"So, three umphs might mean three cheers."

"And if you're not quite as successful you only give two cheers?"

"You got it!" exclaimed Tc'aarlat. "You're *bi*umphant!"

Jack paused again, this time to wipe his hand across his face. "You're rather scarily starting to make sense," he sighed.

Tc'aarlat grinned. "Well, as you humans like to—"

Suddenly, the floor of the air-conditioning duct fell away beneath them, sending them crashing to the floor in the room below.

As the dust settled around them Jack sat up, wincing as pain exploded down his back.

They appeared to have fallen into some kind of store-room filled with broken slot machines, gaming tables with torn felt covers, and chairs with damaged or missing legs.

Thankfully they had missed striking almost all of the items in need of repair in the fall and landed on one of the empty areas of carpet.

"Well," said Tc'aarlat, pushing himself up on his hands. "We made it inside in one piece. How does that make you feel?"

Grimacing, Jack pulled a handful of cracked casino chips from beneath his butt and tossed them aside.

"Monumphant."

Moon of Hann, The Blue Diamond Casino, Stairs To The Roof

Jolio Phisk dropped the feet of the late casino owner, Thavo Domp, and reached around to rub his aching back.

"Come on!" urged Sergeant Randy Barber, a few steps farther up the flight. He'd hooked his hands under Domp's armpits. "You heard Malfic. We've got ten minutes to do this or he'll start shooting the others. One for each minute extra we take, starting with the women."

Phisk sneered. "You must be confusing me with someone who cares."

"What?!" snapped Barber. "You're willing to let the others die?"

"So long as it's not me he's murdering."

Barber's lips curled into a snarl. "Persha's ass!" he spat. "You're fucking despicable!"

The high priest pointed an accusing finger in Barber's direction. "Blasphemy!" he cried. "You took the goddess's name in vain! It is only right that you now self-sacrifice!"

"Suck my Persha-pounding dick!" growled Barber. "Now pick up your end and let's get this guy up on the roof before I use my badge to carve you a second asshole!"

Reluctantly Phisk did as he was told, grunting as he lifted Domp's feet and the pair continued up the stairs.

"Seven minutes," announced Barber as they staggered through the fire exit onto the casino's rooftop. Carrying the corpulent corpse to the edge, they heaved it onto the low wall separating them from the four-story drop to the pavement.

Breathing hard, Phisk leaned over the side and waved his arms wide. "Hey!" he yelled. "Up here!"

Barber dragged him away from the edge. "What the fuck are you doing?!"

"Don't you get it?" hissed Phisk. "This is our chance to escape! If we can attract their attention, they can call the fire department or get a ladder or something."

"And leave the others behind?"

"Don't start on that again!" chided Phisk. "It's a dog-eat-dog moon out there, officer, and I do not intend to end up dead on a ledge like this fat fucker!"

Working hard to control his temper, Sergeant Barber grabbed one of Phisk's wrists, spun him around, and twisted his arm up behind his back.

"OW!" yelled the high priest. "What the fuck are you doing?"

"Saving lives!" growled the cop into Phisk's ear. "We've now got less than ninety seconds to get back to the office. If so much as a single hair on one of those girls' heads has been harmed when we get there, I'll tell Malfic you called his mother a flat-titted, ball-sucking whore. You hear me?"

Grimacing with pain, Phisk nodded his compliance.

"Good," snarled Barber. "Now move!"

Sergeant Randy Barber paused just long enough to shove Thavo Domp's corpse over the edge of the roof as commanded before marching his fellow hostage back toward the open fire exit.

They had just reached the staircase when they heard a muffled *splat*, followed by the nauseated cries and screams of those gathered below.

Had either of the men glanced into the shadows to their right as they hurried back across the casino floor to rejoin the rest of the group, they might have just been able to make out Jack and Tc'aarlat watching them pass from the darkness.

20

Moon of Hann, Outside The Blue Diamond Casino

Chief Bis Pargo stared unblinking at the body of Thavo Domp on the sidewalk across the street.

He hadn't noticed the skirmish on the roof that had led to the establishment's owner going over the edge, but he'd been looking directly at the locked doors of The Blue Diamond Casino when Domp had hit the ground right in front of them.

He'd seen the body burst on impact.

Domp striking the ground had sounded like a side of meat being slapped onto the counter by a careless butcher.

Despite standing on the opposite side of the road, he'd felt some kind of wet, warm fluid spray his face.

What the fluid was he didn't know, nor did he want to. Blood? Bile? Urine? He didn't want to wipe it away, since that would mean acknowledging what he had just witnessed had really happened. And Bis Pargo didn't know if he'd be able to deal with that certainty.

He continued to stare at the corpse—now oozing a rainbow of differently-colored liquids that merged together into a single slowly-spreading brown puddle. Lake began to dab away the spots of wetness from his forehead, cheeks, and lips.

"Th-thank you," he murmured, his eyes beginning to sting from the lack of blinking. "Thank you very..."

The end of the sentence faded away to nothing.

"I think it might be time for you to stand down, sir," said Lake, gently easing his employer into a chair someone had fetched from the Shrillexian restaurant behind them.

The chief resumed blinking, but not with any real enthusiasm.

"Yes," he said softly. "I'll stand down."

"Would you like me to call the negotiator back, sir?" Lake asked. "It might be better if he took over now."

"Trained negotia..." Pargo turned to look at Lake in surprise, as if seeing him for the first time.

"Yes. Yes, I think that might be for the—"

"Bis, darling!" shrieked a female voice so loud and shrill it set Oxbo Lake's teeth on edge. "I got your call, sweetie! Look at you, all in charge!"

Lake's temporary positivity deflated when he saw who was striding toward them, lines of beaming cops parting like waves to allow her access.

Minty Clinch, Hann's most popular—and most irritating—news reporter.

Everything about the woman was fake, from her accent to her pneumatic breasts. She wore false eyelashes, sported dyed pink hair, and pouted wildly through artificially plumped lips.

Behind her scuttled a gorilla of a man with a TV camera on his shoulder and a tall, thin figure wielding a microphone at the end of a pole.

"Mwah! Mwah!" The news anchor kissed the air on either side of Bis Pargo's face, then playfully tapped the end of his nose with one of the long scarlet talons she wore as fingernails.

"I came as quickly as I could, lovekins!" she cawed. "But then, I always do when we get together, don't I?!"

Tossing back her head, she projected a loud raucous laugh which to Oxbo Lake sounded like someone clubbing a bistok to death with a hammer.

Neither her camera ape nor her sound-stick reacted in any way.

"So what's going on, honey pie? What have you got for me this time?"

Pargo opened his mouth to reply but Clinch pressed a finger to his lips to hush him, her wide eyes fixed on the corpse across the street.

"Is that Thavo Domp?" she squealed excitedly. "I've rarely seen him looking so photogenic! Boys, I want close-ups of the body from all angles. Get as much coverage as you can over there while I have a little *tête-à-tête* with Poppa Bear!"

"No, you can't—" exclaimed Oxbo Lake, reaching out to stop them as the camera crew made their way across the street to film the remains of the casino owner. No one paid him any attention.

Delving into her bistok-hide purse, Minty Clinch produced a notepad with a glitter-coated cover and a golden pen. "OK, stud!" she cooed, flicking through the pad to reach a blank page. "Spill it!"

The change in the police chief's attitude was astounding. Gone was any sign of the nervous out-of-his-depth milksop who had only a few moments earlier wanted nothing more than to scurry back to the safety of his warm and corpse-free office.

The bloated blowhard was back in full force.

"Minty, you're just in time to witness the future mayor of this moon in action, personally leading a SWAT team to storm The Blue Diamond Casino, free the terrified hostages and slap the cuffs on a violent serial-killing bastard!"

Somewhere beneath several thick layers of makeup Minty Clinch's face lit up with delight. "How thrilling! Can we come with you?"

"Of course!" crowed Pargo, turning to his horrified assistant. "Lake, give the SWAT team the order to suit up, get me the biggest gun you can find in the armorer's truck, and fetch Miss Clinch a bullet-proof vest!"

"Something figure-hugging, babe!" mewed the reporter, cupping her rock-solid breasts. "I want to be sure to show these puppies off to their very best advantage. They cost me a damn fortune, after all!"

Moon of Hann, Inside The Blue Diamond Casino

Jack and Tc'aarlat pressed themselves against the wall on the landing in front of the late gaming impresario's office. By finding the correct angle, they could use the reflection from the mirrored wall behind the bar to watch

Vimor Malfic pace up and down before his remaining hostages.

Both men drew their modified Jean Dukes Specials.

"What do we set them to?" hissed Tc'aarlat.

Jack turned his dial slowly, matching each *click* with the rhythmic sounds emanating from the slot machines on the casino floor below.

"Stun only," he replied. "I want both Malfic and Phisk alive, and we have to be careful not to wing any of the innocents in there when it all kicks off."

"Innocents!" spat Tc'aarlat. "Can you really call anyone who comes to this butt-crack of a moon 'innocent?'"

"You know, for a former smuggler and money-launderer for the mob you come across as extremely judgmental sometimes."

"Hey!" exclaimed Tc'aarlat. "That hurts! And I'm willing to bet you've not led a squeaky-clean life yourself. I can see you being a pervert in the course of justice."

"What?!" Jack scowled. "No, that's wrong. The phrase is 'pervert the course of justice'!"

"That's what I said!" countered Tc'aarlat. "You're just as much of a pervert as I am!"

Jack sighed. "Forget it! What's the plan?"

Tc'aarlat shrugged. "Never come back here?"

"No, you crusted cretin!" whispered Jack, gesturing to the office door. "What's the plan once we get in there?!"

"Oh," replied Tc'aarlat. "No idea. I was going to follow your lead."

"And what if I haven't got a lead?"

"Then I guess we're fucked."

Jack rubbed the bridge of his nose. "Okay, now let's imagine we don't *want* to get fucked..."

"Sounds good to me."

"So, what's the twatting plan?!"

Before the Yollin could respond, the screen of his wrist communicator lit up and Solo's face appeared. "Excuse me, Tc'aarlat," she began at full volume. "Is Captain Marber with you? I need to get—"

Tc'aarlat tore the device off his arm and hurled it as far as he could across the casino floor.

But it was too late. The office door beside the two men was wrenched open and the barrel of a gun was pressed to the side of Tc'aarlat's head.

"Toss your weapons, fuck-nuggets!"

Tc'aarlat glanced at Jack, who nodded. Reluctantly, the two men threw their guns down the staircase, sending them clattering to the floor of the gaming room below.

"Well, well!" snarled Vimor Malfic. "Looks like we've got a couple of heroes sneaking up on us."

"There's no way we'd have a go at anyone, buddy," commented Tc'aarlat. "We can't even agree on a plan."

Malfic struck the Yollin hard across the side of his face with the gun, knocking him backward.

CRUNCH!

Jack caught his friend before he could tumble down the stairs.

"You two...inside, *now!*"

Jack and Tc'aarlat were marched into the room. The hostages looked at them with hope in their eyes...which quickly drained away once they realized that the two newcomers weren't accompanied by any form of back-up and that their captor clearly had the drop on them.

Tc'aarlat made to join the other hostages along the far wall.

"No, no, no!" growled Malfic. "You two, kneel!"

Tc'aarlat stopped and slowly turned to face the felon. Two steps took him back to the center of the room, where he planned to glare directly back at his aggressor.

Unfortunately he found himself staring hard at Malfic's chest.

Angling his head up, he snarled at the hostage-taker's chin.

"I don't kneel for anyone!" he snapped.

CRUNCH!

The Yollin received a second strike across his face with Malfic's gun in return for his comment.

"Maybe you didn't hear me, fuckwit—"

CRUNCH!

"I said I don't—"

CRUNCH!

"Kneel for—"

CRUNCH!

"Anyone!"

CRUNCH!

Tc'aarlat blinked back the blood dripping into his right eye from a cut just above it.

"However, on this occasion I'm prepared to make an exception."

The Yollin sank slowly to his knees beside Jack. He attempted to offer his colleague a conspiratorial wink but could only twitch his already half-closed eye.

Malfic pressed the barrel of his gun to Tc'aarlat's forehead. "You think you're a funny fucker, don't you?"

This time, Tc'aarlat didn't reply.

"I don't like funny fuckers."

Still nothing.

"But I do like turning them into dead fuckers!"

He thumbed back the hammer.

Tc'aarlat closed both his good and bad eyes.

This was it.

This is where it was going to end.

After years of working for, then ripping off the mob, chasing down Dark Tomorrow terrorists, and now spying for the *Etheric Federation*, it all came down to this.

Being executed by an escaped convict in a cheap casino on a sleazy moon.

Fucking wonderful.

Tc'aarlat concentrated on the circle of metal against his forehead. "You'd better make sure you have enough firepower in that thing to get through my exoskeleton," he spat. "'Cos if you don't kill me with the first shot, I'm gonna stuff my fist down your throat and rip out your fucking lungs."

"Oh, I've got the firepower," snarled Malfic.

Then came the gunshot.

For a moment, all Tc'aarlat knew was silence. Was this what came next? Was this how it all happened? Just silence?

Gradually, he came to realize he wasn't cocooned in silence. There was noise. So much noise, his brain must have temporarily severed the connection to his ears to prevent serious damage.

And the noise felt hot! How could that be? He could smell it, too. It smelled like burning flesh.

Then everything came rushing back into sharp focus. His ears were ringing, and the smell was burning the inside of his nostrils.

He was still alive.

Malfic had dropped his gun and staggered back against the far wall, his left hand pressed over a blast wound that had taken out part of his right shoulder.

The ringing was the result of a shot crashing past his head. Someone had arrived just in time to shoot Malfic and save his life.

The Yollin stood shakily, turning to see who it was.

Oh no.

Oh, fucking NO!

Not him!

Anyone but HIM!

"Bet you thought we weren't coming, huh?" grinned Draven.

"NO!" screamed Tc'aarlat, snatching up Malfic's weapon. "Do it again!" he roared, charging over to the wounded felon and trying to force the gun back into his limp, useless hand. "DO IT AGAIN!"

Then someone was dragging him away. No, not one person. Two. He looked up, his good eye swimming with tears of frustration. Jack had hold of one arm and Adina had the other.

They were dragging him back toward the door.

And still that damn ringing pierced his damn mind! What the fuck had Draven shot Malfic with, a *Gott Verdammt* cannon?"

Fighting free of his fellow Shadows, Tc'aarlat stood and scanned the room for the pin-up pilot.

There he was! And he was clutching a...

"What the shit *is* that thing?!" he demanded.

Draven waved what looked like a meter-long Jean Dukes Special. It was a fucking monster of a gun.

"The latest thing to come from the labs back home," he explained. "They call it 'The Thunderbolt.'"

Tc'aarlat spun to look at Jack for his reaction and saw another of the stunning new weapons in Adina's hands.

"Draven brought them with him in the new *Pegasus*," she told him. "There's one for you back on the ship. We get to keep them."

She handed her colleagues their JD Specials. "Callis found these on the casino floor," she said. "We thought you might like them back."

From just outside the office doorway, Callis gave a shy wave.

Tc'aarlat lifted his hands, a gun in each. One, some shitty point-and-shoot piece of crap that Malfic was planning to execute him with, the other his trusted Jean Dukes Special.

He dumped the lesser weapon on the couch between the two female hostages. They clung to each other, with Lowlon Quell, Zalah Gilt, and Jolio Phisk hovering nearby.

Sergeant Barber was missing, presumably having gone to unlock the casino doors and call in assistance.

"You okay?" Jack asked the Yollin.

Tc'aarlat nodded, wiping the blood still pooling around his injured eye with the back of his hand.

"Never better." He spun the dial on his weapon, his gaze fixed firmly on the slumped figure of Vimor Malfic.

Three. Four. Five. Six.

Seven.

He began to walk across the office toward the serial killer.

"Whoa!" cried Jack, grabbing his arm. "What the fuck are you doing?"

Tc'aarlat yanked his arm free.

And kept walking.

Malfic looked up, his eyes struggling to focus as they met Tc'aarlat's. The felon's breathing was growing increasingly shallow as blood pumped from his wounded shoulder.

He wouldn't last much longer at this rate.

And Tc'aarlat wasn't going to let him go that easily.

He could hear Jack shouting his name somewhere in the distance; somewhere beyond the fierce ringing and the cries of relief from the few remaining hostages.

But he ignored it all.

Slowly he raised his gun, pressing the end of the barrel hard against Malfic's sweat-covered forehead.

"Hello," he said calmly. "The funny fucker's back."

Then a smoke grenade landed in the middle of the room and exploded.

Reality turned to shit again. People ran, screamed, coughed, puked.

Tc'aarlat saw figures moving into the room. Figures dressed in dark clothing. Figures wearing full-face gas masks.

The police.

"Down on the floor! I said, get down on the floor!"

At first the Yollin couldn't work out why he was being manhandled like this. Why he was being pushed face first onto the carpet. Why some damn mountain of a cop was sitting on his fucking back!

He was one of the good guys.

Then a heavy black boot stamped down on his wrist and his gun was pulled from his hand.

Shit! They thought he was one of the hostage takers!

Twisting his head to one side, he found he wasn't alone on the ground. Jack was lying to his left. Adina and Draven were on his right.

They were all shouting something, but he couldn't make out what it was.

Fuck this fucking ringing in his fucking ears!

Then the smoke began to dissipate. Members of the SWAT team pulled off their masks.

A new figure strode confidently into the room, squeezed into a bullet-proof vest that barely contained his expansive stomach. It was the police chief who had fucked them off outside the casino.

Followed by what appeared to be a hairless ape with a camera, some rake-thin streak of nothing almost invisible behind his mic pole, and a pouting plastic tart covered in enough make-up to stock a department store.

"Yes!" Chief Bis Pargo beamed. "I think that all went extremely well!"

"Consider yourself headline news, darling!" tooted the tart with the titanic tracks of land.

And still Tc'aarlat couldn't make out what Jack was shouting. He had to silence the room.

"YYYAAAAAARRRRGGGGHHHHH!" he roared.

Everyone else fell silent for a moment.

Everyone but Jack.

"Where is he?" he was screaming. "Where the fuck is he?!"

The reality of the situation hit Tc'aarlat like a diamond sledgehammer. He forced himself up, although the large cop was still sitting on him.

Finally, he had enough movement to turn and look at the blood-smeared wall behind him.

That was all there was. Just the wall and the blood.

Vimor Malfic was missing.

21

Moon of Hann, Backstreets

Sergeant Randy Barber drew the gun he'd borrowed from a colleague outside the casino and approached the corner of the dark street.

He'd spotted Vimor Malfic disappearing through the crowds while giving his immediate superior details of what had transpired during the siege and had quickly followed, pausing only to ask a friend on the force for the loan of his weapon.

Even here, several streets away from the main drag, the constant mixture of sounds blasting from the many businesses touting their wares to tourists could still be heard, albeit mellowed into a low-level white noise by the distance.

If it weren't for the fact that he was on the trail of a malicious serial killer who had slaughtered at least two individuals before his eyes, Barber might have found it comforting.

Forcing the aural distraction to the back of his mind, Barber paused just long enough to allow his eyes to adjust to the subtle street lighting. Flickering aged bulbs cast islands of yellow light here and there among the vast ocean of forbidding darkness.

Darkness which seemed to invite shady underhanded dealings. Although, with gambling, drugs and prostitution being offered freely and legally to one and all as mere pastimes in the more frequented areas of town, only police officers like Barber knew just how shady and underhanded things could really get in Hann's dim alleys and backstreets.

Once the swirling purple and green aftershocks of the main strip's neon gaudiness had melted away, Barber continued onward. He knew Malfic was injured and bleeding, so there was a possibility he might leave a trail of blood behind as he slithered into the night.

The challenge was to differentiate between splashes of fresh blood and the dried puddles of life-force spilled by other defiled denizens of these ghastly, grim ghettoes.

Suddenly, a sound!

Barber froze, listening hard; trying to separate what he'd just heard from the scratch and scrape of rats' claws and the beleaguered breathing of a trio of tramps on the next corner sleeping off whatever concoction of chemicals was coursing through their veins.

There it was again.

Footsteps.

He could hear footsteps.

The slow dragging of feet that could denote a man battling weakness through loss of blood, fighting to remain conscious in the knowledge that his escape plan was not yet complete.

That there was still time for his sudden freedom to be brought abruptly and permanently to an end.

Sergeant Barber allowed himself a brief smile. He was on Malfic's trail at last. Playing by the rules had once again proved to be the right thing to do. As always, the good guy was going to win.

It was most likely due to this moment of confidence that he didn't hear his attacker until the blade of his knife was already sliding across the front of his throat.

Moon of Hann, Outside The Blue Diamond Casino

"And where the fuck do you think *you're* going?" demanded Draven as he dragged Jolio Phisk from the doorway of the dungeon in which police officers were continuing to take statements.

"I'm going with the others," replied Phisk, clearly flustered. "Chief Pargo wants to debrief me on what happened in there."

"I'm more concerned about what happened back on Taglen," replied Draven. "To be more specific, back at the Temple of Persha."

Phisk pulled his arm free. "Do you know who I am?"

Draven nodded. "Even worse, I know *what* you are."

"Oh, and what's that?"

"A killer," responded Draven.

"How dare you!"

"And a coward," added Draven. "You don't even have the guts to murder your victims yourself. Instead, you guilt your victims into committing 'self-sacrifice,' or as the rest of the civilized universe likes to call it, suicide. All in the name of some imagined deity."

Phisk's expression darkened. "The Goddess Persha—"

"Is an excuse for your despicable behavior," Draven finished. "Religion may have saved Taglen from civil war, but it also replaced the corrupt politicians with the likes of you. Perverted priests out to fill their pockets and empty their balls in the name of the twin goddesses."

"You claim Persha is imagined?"

Draven shrugged. "Whether gods exist isn't for me to say. What *is* imagined is that they speak through ass-wipes like you, and that their laws just happen to benefit the chosen few able to 'hear' their unspoken commands."

Phisk fell silent for a moment, staring down his nose at Draven as if he were something he had just wiped from the bottom of his shoe.

"You are not even from Taglen," he said at last. "Who are you to presume to judge me?"

Draven slapped his palm against his forehead. "Jeez, you're right! I guess I don't get a say in this after all."

"Finally," grumbled Phisk, turning away, "you've said something that makes a little sense. Now, if you will excuse me..."

Click!

The high priest spun back, staring down at the handcuff his accuser had fastened around one of his wrists.

"However..." said Draven, grabbing Phisk's other arm and securing the other cuff. "We did place a call to a couple of judges down on Taglen, and they were very interested to learn just how much of the church's collections have ended up in the tills of, shall we say, less-than-pious establishments here on Hann. And they'd really like to discuss all that with you at your earliest convenience."

"What? But I..."

Draven pushed the now-handcuffed Jolio Phisk in the direction of the nearest police vehicle. "Time to say your prayers, Father Fuckball!"

On the other side of the police cruiser, Tc'aarlat sat on the back step of an ambulance while a paramedic stitched up the cut above his right eye.

"OW!" he yelled, wincing as the medic stabbed him with the fifth needle he'd used during what should have been a simple procedure. "Watch it, fella! That hurts!"

"It's not my fault the needles keep snapping on your exoskeleton," countered the paramedic. "I'm down to the last few in my kit, and they're thicker and blunter than the others."

"Would it help if I held your hand?" asked Callis, sitting beside the Yollin. From her perch on the teen's shoulder, Mist shrieked loudly.

SKAAWWWWW!

Tc'aarlat met and held the paramedic's gaze for a moment, then whispered to Callis, "Yes. Please."

As the pair linked fingers, Tc'aarlat looked at his raal hawk. "She's still green."

Callis nodded. "She has been all the while I've had her. What do you think it means?"

"I really don't know," admitted Tc'aarlat with a small sigh. "But I'm worried in case she's feeling— OW! FUCK-FUCK*FUCK*FUCK*!"

"Sorry!" muttered the paramedic. "Almost finished!"

Deedee Joh glanced at the ambulance as Tc'aarlat's cursing reached her ears, and she shivered. Normally the only place she stood while dressed in her sequined bikini was beneath the hot air blower across the top of the entrance to the casino.

The outfit wasn't designed to be worn elsewhere.

Someone carefully placed a jacket around her shoulders.

"Oh, it's you!" said Deedee, looking up to find Zalah Gilt smiling down at her. "Thank you, that's very kind."

"Don't think about it," Gilt smiled. "Crazy night, huh?"

Deedee snorted a laugh. "And my last!"

Gilt frowned. "What?"

The door girl looked at her boss as if he were crazy. "If you think I'm coming back here again after all this, you're crazier than the fools who bet their hard-earned cash beyond those doors. My days of smiling at fat handsy businessmen and college kids are *over*!"

"What if you didn't have to smile at them?" asked Gilt.

"What you talkin' about?"

"Well," continued the floor manager, "what if you could arrange things for them, or kick them out when they're getting too rowdy or, as you say, 'handsy' with the girls at the door."

Deedee scowled. "That sounds a lot like *your* job."

"It is," replied Gilt. "Or at least it was. Now that Mr. Domp is...not with us any longer, this place will most likely pass into the hands of whoever owns the largest number of shares."

"And that person is?"

Zalah Gilt bowed. "Sixty-two percent, at your service."

He beamed. "I've used just about every single paycheck to buy 'em up one or two shares at a time for over a decade now."

Deedee glanced back at the casino, which was now swarming with crime-scene investigators is matching white jumpsuits. "You're the new owner of that nasty ol' dump?"

"One and the same," agreed Gilt. "And that dump needs a new floor manager now I've taken the bold move of promoting myself."

Smiling, Deedee Joh linked arms with her boss. "What say we continue this conversation after you buy me a couple drinks and a big 'ol steak?!"

The pair turned, almost bumping into Lowlon Quell as he stumbled along the sidewalk. The effects of the vast amount of alcohol he'd consumed earlier in the evening had combined with the fumes from the smoke grenade to result in the only prize he was taking away from his visit to The Blue Diamond Casino-—a killer headache.

"Hey, Mr. Quell!" called a voice. "Lowlon! Wait up!"

Quell turned to discover Nat Farrow hurrying to catch up with him, still dressed in her smart croupier uniform but now with a dark windbreaker over the top.

"Which way are you heading?" she asked. "Which hotel are you staying in? You need a ride?"

"I *was* at The Regal," answered Quell. "But I doubt I can go back there, even to get my stuff."

"Why not?"

Quell turned out his empty pockets. "I don't have enough to pay the bill for my stay," he grumbled. "I was supposed to check out first thing in the morning, but unless I exit via the fire escape they're likely to spot me at the front desk."

"Oh," said Nat, lowering her gaze. "I'm sorry."

"Not your fault," smiled Quell. "You can only deal the cards in the order they're stacked."

"That's not strictly true," admitted Nat with an expression of guilt. "Mr. Domp owns the company that makes and packages the playing cards we use. He has them arranged in a sequence that works against the players."

The conquered cardsharp let loose a grunt of frustration.

"GAH! To think that just a few hours ago I was the owner of a Jackpot Chip! I had a million credits right there in my hands! Do you have any idea how that feels?"

"In a way," said Nat. "My dad owes a lot of money to Mr. Domp. Well, he did. I guess that will have passed to whoever takes over next."

Lowlon Quell wrapped an arm around her shoulders. "Well, if I still had that chip I'd make certain his debt was paid," he insisted. "You're the only person who's not out to get me drunk, rip me off, or shoot me in the face since I landed on this blasted excuse for a moon."

Nat glanced up and down the street. "That Jackpot Chip..." She smiled. "Did it look a little like this?"

The croupier reached into her pocket and pulled out a bright-blue chip with a diamond-shaped logo etched on the front.

"You took one!" gasped Quell, his eyes large.

"Of course not!" Nat scolded sternly, producing a second identical chip. "I took two! One each."

Lowlon Quell's mouth opened and closed as the

croupier handed one of the chips to him, but no sound came out.

Nat beamed. "I figured I was due a raise after what happened tonight—not that I'll be working there again after all this."

"But... But... We can't go back there to cash them in, can we?"

"No need," said the croupier conspiratorially. "All the casinos on Hann have signed a chip transfer policy. We can swap these bad boys for cold hard cash just about anywhere!"

"Then what are we waiting for?" Quell grinned. "Let's go celebrate!

Hand in hand, the pair raced off along the street, ducking under the boom microphone dangling above the bleached-blonde head of Minty Clinch as she crooned a piece to camera about how the moon's visitors from the *Etheric Federation* had ended the hostage situation.

"And so, the business owners of Hann owe these men and women a huge debt of gratitude for everything they have done," she concluded.

Making a "cut" gesture, Minty turned away from the camera. "Get that edited and ready for the next bulletin," she commanded her two-man team. "Then come back in case the producer wants to do a live link-up with the studio."

The gargantuan camera operator grunted his agreement and the two men marched away with their equipment.

As they vacated the spot beside their boss, Chief Bis Pargo quickly sidled up to fill it.

"So..." he said in as seductive a voice as he could emit. "How about a one-on-one with the guy in charge around here? An interview with the real power figure on Hann..."

Minty Clinch's false eyelashes fluttered. "Capital idea, darling!" she cooed. "I saw him just a moment ago... Wait, yes! There he is!"

Her ridiculously high heels played a staccato rhythm against the sidewalk as she scurried over to plant a wet kiss on the cheek of a very surprised Oxbo Lake.

"The man in charge!" she exclaimed loudly. "The power behind the throne, so to speak! What say you and I go somewhere quieter and have a little *tête-à-tête*, huh?"

The bemused publicist blinked hard, nodding as he allowed himself to be led to the entrance of the Shrillexian restaurant.

Pargo's face turned a deep shade of purple. "Barber!" he roared. "With me, now!"

Mike Janely, the officer who had loaned his gun to Barber, hurried across to Pargo. "The sergeant isn't here at the moment, sir!"

"What?" spat Pargo. "Well, I'll deal with him later."

"Yes, sir!"

"In the meantime, get me those interlopers from the *Etheric*-Fucking-*Federation!*"

"At once, sir!" cried Janely, scanning the crowd. He could see one member of the group being attended to by paramedics while the young girl held his hand, and there was another in the process of transferring a handcuffed suspect into the custody of a local officer. But that left two others— the guy who appeared to be in charge, and the woman.

They were nowhere to be seen.

Moon of Hann, Back Streets

Jack and Adina crept down the alleyway, each clutching a Jean Dukes Thunderbolt.

Like the Specials strapped to their sides, the Thunderbolts had the facility to be dialed up or down depending on the ferocity of discharge required by the user.

Each currently had their weapon set to six.

"You're certain Malfic came this way?" hissed Adina.

Jack shook his head. "No, but if I was trying to stay one step ahead of the cops and find a ship off of this rock, this is where *I'd* go."

Coming to a corner, they silently checked if the street was clear in both directions before continuing.

After the near-blinding lights and pounding music of the tourist area, the silence blanketing these backstreets felt heavy and oppressive. As if everything were covered with a thick layer of wool.

Every single sound, from the chittering of the moon's cockroach-like insects, to the buzzing of the street lights, seemed to be amplified by the inky-black darkness all around them.

Then they heard it.

A new sound. A different sound.

A disturbing sound.

Turning the next corner, they found the source and aimed their Thunderbolts directly at it.

On the opposite side of the street was Vimor Malfic,

blood still oozing from his injured shoulder appearing black under the artificial yellow light from above.

His good arm was wrapped around another figure—a figure whose throat and chest was smeared with the same thick, black substance.

As was the blade of the knife in Malfic's hand.

The figure forced his head up and looked at them drowsily.

It was Sergeant Barber!

Like his assailant, he had lost a lot of blood.

He too was growing weaker by the second.

"I'm not going back!" slurred Malfic over Barber's shoulder. "Not to jail. Not with you."

"The choice isn't yours to make," called Jack.

"Yes, it is!" spat Malfic. "You can either let me go or I'll kill you both, just like I'm going to kill this guy!"

"We can't do that," replied Adina. "Let the officer go and we'll get you some help for your shoulder."

Malfic laughed, resting his head against the wall behind him as if the effort of holding it up added to his exhaustion.

"He's not walking away from here!"

Jack peered down the sights of his gun. "Then neither are you, Malfic."

The felon's fingers tightened around the handle of his knife.

"Drop it!" yelled Adina.

Malfic moved the blade closer to Barber's injured throat.

"I said drop it, now!"

Barber winced as he felt the tip of the knife dig into the flesh inside the already-open wound.

Forcing his eyes open as wide as he could, he locked his gaze on Jack. "Do it," he croaked thinly.

Jack's finger played against the trigger of his weapon. "You sure?"

Barber nodded slowly. "Do it."

As Malfic pushed the knife deeper into Barber's throat, both Jack and Adina fired their Thunderbolts, ending the hunt for Vimor Malfic.

22

ICS Fortitude, Bridge

Jack Marber spun in his chair, planning to check that every member of the Shadows was wearing a seatbelt. After everything he'd been through in the past twenty-four hours, he didn't think he could take another dressing-down from Solo.

"OK, before I ask Solo to—"

He stopped short when he realized that Tc'aarlat and Adina were crying.

Jack glanced at Draven in the pull-down seat. Even he was wiping tears from his eyes.

"Have I missed something?" he asked, giving Solo the signal to take off.

Adina dragged a clump of tissues from her pocket. "I'm okay," she sniffed. "It's just that I'm going to miss Callis."

Jack offered her a comforting smile. "We all are," he said as the ship's boosters kicked in and lifted them off the ground. "She's a great kid, and I think she's going to be just fine."

They had left the teenager behind on Taglen after returning to hand Jolio Phisk over to the authorities. Dabriel Yagash, now promoted to High Priest of the Temple of Persha, had agreed to testify at Phisk's trial.

Dabriel had a lot of work to do rebuilding the public's trust in the Church and had enlisted the help of Corlon Strumm in order to make that happen.

Callis had asked to stay once she'd met Dabriel's daughter Hamble. The teen had fallen for the child big time, claiming she was the little sister she'd been deprived of when her parents had sold her into slavery.

Dabriel had happily accepted Adina's suggestion that Callis stay with him as Hamble's full-time nanny. While she didn't want to abandon the girl on the first planet they came to, she knew she would be happy within that community.

And the Shadows would have a set of eyes on the ground, ready to contact them if the big reform plan wasn't followed as agreed.

However, while saying goodbye to Callis answered why Adina was feeling tearful, it didn't explain what had upset the two men so much—although he had a suspicion the cause of Draven's upset was also based on Taglen.

Returning to the *Fortitude* after finding and killing Vimor Malfic, Jack had discovered the body of Merfel Strumm in the ship's cold-storage room. When they had flown back to the planet to return the woman's remains to her husband, Draven had asked to be the one to make the delivery.

He'd been gone for several hours, comforting Corlon Strumm and helping him make arrangements for his wife's funeral. Draven had tried to make the distraught man understand that he wasn't responsible for Merfel's death, or at least not completely. Like the rest of the congregation, he'd been under the Jolio Phisk's spell and had done his bidding.

Draven also explained how he, Adina, and Callis had destroyed The Plant, ensuring no other corpse would enter the food chain. This meant Merfel's death would not be in vain. She had been the reason the trio had visited The Plant in the first place. If it weren't for her, its diabolical machinery might well be up and running still.

That just left Tc'aarlat, and that was going to be a difficult question to ask. In all the time Jack had known the Yollin, the only time he'd ever really opened up was on the journey to Hann in the *Pegasus II*. Now Tc'aarlat was openly weeping on the bridge.

Had he somehow broken his friend and business partner?

Jack glanced at the viewscreen. The ship was approaching Taglen's upper atmosphere and the sky outside was fading from bright- to navy-blue.

Maybe he should wait until he and Tc'aarlat were alone before he broached the subject of why—

ALARMS!

Once again, lights and sirens exploded into life all around the ship.

"Incoming!" exclaimed Solo, appearing on every available screen. "We have another incoming missile!"

"What the fuck?!" cried Jack, spinning back to his control panel. "Solo, take evasive maneuvers!"

"Yes, Captain. I—"

"No need!" yelled Draven, unclipping his safety belt. "I'm on it!"

"Draven!" shouted Solo over the blaring alarms. "Sit down and refasten your safety harness at once!"

But Draven was already pounding along the corridor that led to the rear cargo bay and the hidden hangar.

Without a word, Tc'aarlat unfastened his belt and raced after him.

"*Gott Verdammt!*" spat Jack. "Not this shit again!"

Solo's avatar scowled on-screen. "Tc'aarlat, please return to your— Jack! Adina! Where do you two think you are going? Return to your seats!"

"Sorry, Solo, not this time!" cried Jack as he ran from the bridge with Adina at his heels. "I've got to stop this ridiculous rivalry before someone gets hurt—or worse!"

The alarms continued to scream as Jack and Adina raced for the rear hangar, the corridor pitching from side to side as Solo worked to keep the ship out of the missile's trajectory.

They reached the hangar just in time to see the *Pegasus II* blast off from the rear of the ship, flying straight for the approaching projectile as it twisted and turned in the air, following the *Fortitude*'s every move.

"Pair of fucking idiots!" barked Jack. "Solo! Can you take control of the *Pegasus* and return her to the *Fortitude*?"

"I'm afraid not, Captain," came Solo's reply from a speaker embedded in the wall. "Manual flight has been activated and locked. I could try to break through and override it, but it would take some time."

"We don't *have* time!" put in Adina, "but try anyway!"

"Certainly."

Jack paced as the shuttle ducked and dived, mimicking the missile's movement as it flew closer and closer.

"What are they doing?" he demanded. "They've got weapons! Why aren't they blasting the fucking thing into tiny pieces?"

"I'm afraid that won't be possible, Captain," announced Solo. "According to my readings, all weapons on board the *Pegasus II* have jammed."

"Jammed? How?"

"The problem seems to have occurred when I used the *Fortitude*'s rear thrusters to detonate the previous missile," explained Solo. "The resulting heat blast appears to have melted the housing for the gun turrets in addition to removing the paint on the front end."

"Wait!" sputtered Jack. "They're out there without any firepower? Then how the fuck are they going to stop—"

BOOM!

The explosion knocked both Jack and Adina off their feet.

Shielding his eyes from the fiery glare, Jack crawled over to where Adina lay.

"Are you all right?"

"I think so," Adina replied with a cough. "What happened?"

Jack peered into space. Behind the ship, the bright orange and yellow fireball made possible only by the surplus oxygen in the *Fortitude*'s exhaust was now dissipating.

"They flew right into it."

Adina sat up, her eyes growing wet with tears once again. "*What?*"

Jack nodded, turning around to sit beside her. "They're gone," he murmured. "They saved us."

Behind the ship, spinning shards of metal were being caught in the pale blue jets erupting from the *Fortitude*'s engines.

All that was left of the *Pegasus II* was a slowly rotating clump of twisted, burned metal.

"How the fuck are we going to tell Nathan about this?" asked Jack.

"How the fuck are we going to tell him we lost another *Pegasus*?" queried a voice from behind them.

Jack and Adina spun.

Tc'aarlat was standing in the entrance to the hangar holding a cardboard box.

"But... But..." Jack staggered to his feet. "You ran after Draven to get in the *Pegasus* with him!"

"Like fuck I did!" countered Tc'aarlat. "The man's a walking suicide mission, as he's just proven."

Adina took Jack's hand and clambered up to stand beside him. "Then where did you go?"

Tc'aarlat nodded to the cardboard box in his hands. According to the logo printed on the side it had once contained cans of vegetable soup. Now the lid had been folded back over the top to conceal whatever was currently inside.

"I figured out why Mist turned green," explained the Yollin.

Jack and Adina crossed the hangar as Tc'aarlat folded back the box's lid. There, lying securely in a nest-shaped mound of shredded paper and cable-ties, were three pink eggs.

Adina gasped. "She... But how? When?"

Tc'aarlat shrugged. "Back on Damkin prime, I guess," he said, tears running down his cheeks again. "I'm going to be a granddad!"

"I'm not entirely sure that's how it works," came a familiar voice through the wall speaker.

"Draven!" yelled Jack, spinning to peer at the shrinking hunk of blasted metal. "You lived through that?"

"Depends on what you call living," Draven replied. "I've got multiple fractures, a couple of snapped ribs, one of my lungs has been punctured, and I'm not likely to see my spleen again anytime soon."

"You're still inside the shuttle?!" questioned Adina.

"Not much of a shuttle anymore, but yeah. Any chance of a ride home?"

"Adina, with me!" shouted Jack, running toward the bridge. Adina paused long enough to take another peek inside the box, then she planted a kiss on Tc'aarlat's cheek and gave chase.

Alone, the Yollin peered out the rear doors as the ICS *Fortitude* began to bank to starboard. Solo was obviously following orders to turn around so they could collect the wreckage of the *Pegasus II* and Draven.

Glancing down at the three eggs, he smiled.

"One thing you should know about your Uncle Draven,

kids... He doesn't have a bad bone in his body, but that doesn't mean he won't make you want to break every single fucking one of them!"

"Oh," added the Yollin, his expression now serious, "and don't let on to Jack or Adina that I know exactly who's been firing missiles at us."

FINIS

The Shadows will return in
SHADOW VANGUARD 3:
IMMORTALITY CURSE

BONUS SCENE

Wonder what happened just before this adventure started? Here's a bonus scene for all you fans of the Shadows, where the team meets a few familiar faces...

Adina Choudhury stretched her neck from side to side as she led the way out of the White Orchid Spa tucked behind a promenade shop and sighed happily.

"Oh, I feel much better after that!" she proclaimed to the tall figure catching up with her. "Didn't I tell you a little bit of pampering would do us all some good?"

Captain Jack Marber pressed his hands against the small of his back and nodded. "You did indeed," he said. ". They're very good in there. Months of backache from sitting in the *Fortitude*'s crappy pilot seat— – gone. We have to do this more often. I feel great!"

"Speak for yourself," moaned the Yollin following them

through the door. "I still feel like I've gone ten rounds with a Shrillexian kick-boxer."

He rolled his shoulders, the joints popping noisily, causing the blood red raal hawk perched beside his right ear to let out an irritated SQUAWWW!

Jack offered Adina a sly wink. "Don't say we didn't warn you," he commented. "Life-forms with exoskeletons shouldn't get massages."

"That poor guy," added Adina, her expression becoming serious. "I hope the damage to his wrists doesn't keep him off work for too long."

"I doubt it," said Jack. "Once the medic had finished bandaging the cuts and bruises on his hands, he reckoned the masseur would be fine after a few weeks of physio-therapy."

"Well, he'd better not blame any of that on me," grunted Tc'aarlat. "I offered to go get the toolbox from the ship so he could really go to town on me, but he refused, saying he had a few dicks up his sleeve."

"I think you mean he had 'a few tricks' up his sleeve," corrected an amused voice from behind the group.

The trio turned to find a familiar figure approaching, arm outstretched.

"Nathan!" cried Jack, taking the proffered hand and shaking it firmly. "Didn't expect to bump into you on this station."

"I'm just here to drop off TH and Char," Nathan replied, gesturing to the two people with him. Both were tall, well-built, and laden with more than a few shopping bags. "They're due some vacation time, and I suggested they spend it here on Onyx Station."

There was a small buzz, and Nathan pulled his tablet from his pocket. "Excuse me folks, I have to take this," he said, stepping away from the group as his fingers danced across the screen.

The tall man nodded. "If I'd known 'vacation' was code word for shopping I'd have gone on a mission instead," he said. "Give me suicidal aliens and blowing shit up over emptying my account for the privilege of sore feet and a dry mouth any day."

The woman stuck out her tongue and narrowed her striking purple eyes. "Not my fault you're slow on the uptake, Marine!" she teased. "Only three more stores, then I'll let you go for a beer."

"I'll need more than one if this is how you plan to spend the entire vacation," her partner chuckled. He turned to Jack, Adina and Tc'aarlat, holding out his hand. "Terry Henry Walton, but my friends call me TH."

"Jack Marber," replied Jack as they shook, "and this is Adina and Tc'aarlat."

"I'm Char," smiled the woman, setting down her purchases to join in with the handshakes. "I'll be standing here all day if I leave it to TH to introduce me."

"I love your hair!" offered Adina, gazing appreciatively at the silver stripe running down the length of the woman's glossy, dark locks.

"Thanks!" responded Char, running her fingers through the thick tresses. "TH says it's my way of making a statement. But, I've no idea what that statement might be."

"It's your frequently-stated commitment to never knowingly pass an open store without purchasing their entire stock," TH groaned. "You guys want to come and grab that beer with me while the ladies share shopping tips?"

"Beer sounds good," said Tc'aarlat. "And Mist never says no to a dish of muri meat, do you girl?"

The scarlet-feathered raal hawk shrieked her agreement.

SKAWWWWW!

"Unfortunately, we can't," said Jack. "We have an appointment to keep on Damkin Prime; a few bad guys need fucking up due to their ongoing interest in buying and selling child slaves."

"That sounds even more fun than shopping," beamed Char. "Do you want a couple of extra fucker-uppers? TH is a crack shot, and it might be useful to have a werewolf on your side of the equation."

"You're a werewolf?" croaked Adina, taking a small step back.

"As vicious as she is beautiful!" said TH with pride.

"Looks like you two have more in common than just hair and shopping," Tc'aarlat pointed out to Adina. "If we go for that beer, you could learn more about- OW!"

The Yollin bent to his right, rubbing at the spot where Adina's elbow had made contact with his ribs. "*Gott Verdammt!*" he cried. "How come a trained masseur can't make a dent in my exoskeleton, but you can jab me like the horn of a charging bistok?"

"Practice makes perfect – and pain!" Adina snarled, readying her elbow once more.

"I think that's our cue to take our leave," said Jack. He shook TH's and Char's hands again. "Say goodbye to Nathan for us once he's finished his call."

"Sure will," smiled TH.

"And good luck with your slave traders," added Char.

Jack glanced at Adina and Tc'aarlat as they glared angrily at each other. "Judging by the mood these guys are in, I suspect it will be the bad guys who need all the luck!"

AUTHOR NOTES - TOM DUBLIN

MAY 30, 2018

STOP! These author notes contain spoilers for *Shadow Vanguard 2: Lunar Crisis*. If you haven't finished the book yet, do not read this section!

Lunar Crisis was great fun to write.

I had really got to know my three main characters - Captain Jack Marber, Tc'aarlat and Adina Choudhury - very well while writing their first adventure, *Gravity Storm*. But, because I'd had to include the origin story for the Shadows in that book, there had been a limit to just how much action, intrigue and comedy I could include when the story eventually reached the political ins and outs of Alma Nine.

This time, I didn't have to include that set-up. I could hit the ground running, and ramp up the excitement from chapter one.

And that's where things began to surprise me.

You'll occasionally hear an author say that, once things

are flowing well during the writing of a book, that their characters can come to life and act in unexpected ways.

That's exactly what happened to me.

For example, I *knew* we were going to open in the middle of an action sequence. That's something I've always loved about the *James Bond* movies - that we catch up with 007 when he's balls-deep in an ongoing mission.

And so, I had Jack, Adina and Tc'aarlat taking out slave-traders in an assault which would likely have taken an extreme amount of planning. Then, as they head off to return the rescued children to their families, someone fires a couple of missiles at them.

No rest for the wicked.

That much, I expected. I also expected for an *Etheric Federation* pilot - Draven - to deliver a replacement for the destroyed *Pegasus* shuttle to the team, and arrive just in time to save their lives.

However, I DID NOT expect Tc'aarlat to become insanely jealous of Draven. That took me completely by surprise - and I loved it! The scenes with the two of them bickering quickly became my favorite sections to write, and I began to manufacture more ways for Tc'aarlat to try to get one over on his rival, only to fail miserably.

It was great fun!

And then, Solo shocked me.

While penning a scene detailing her quirk of insisting everyone on board fasten their safety belts, she pointed out that the teenage girl hiding in one of the food storage rooms was not strapped in.

WHO?

I genuinely had no idea who the hell Solo was talking

about. I trawled back through all my notes - but there was no such character. So, I had to stop and invent Callis before I could write any further (the moment we catch her peering out of the darkness as the crew offload the other rescued kids was added in later, as a little teaser for the readers).

So, now I had an unexpected relationship between Tc'aarlat and Draven, and a whole new character. Surely it would be smooth sailing from that point onwards.

Yeah, right...

The Shadows landed on Taglen, made their way to the Temple of Persha, met a grieving Corlon Strumm (all planned), and then he goes and blurts out that his deceased wife is going to be chopped up and fed to the poor!

WHAT THE FUCK?!

Which part of my dark and twisted imagination had that sprung from? Again, I had no idea that line was coming, and it changed a lot of the remaining plot. I knew the team would split up, and that Adina would lead her group off in search of Merfel Strumm's corpse - but I didn't know about The Plant, and Jolio Phisk's decree that self-sacrificed sinners were to be used as a food source.

So, another pause, another re-working of my notes.

I finally got back to writing... and Mist turned green.

FFS!

I was aware that I was under-using Mist a little in this adventure; the back and forth between her master and Draven had taken up a lot of space where she was going to play a part. I also knew I wanted to have her change color for some reason, but presumed it would be to help the mission in some way.

Then she faded from red to green - and stayed that way.

Her reason for the change was one of the last things I thought up while writing. I was working on the very last chapter when I realized she was about to lay eggs.

I still have no idea what will happen with that sub-plot in the following books. But, you know what?

I don't care.

I know these strange and unusual characters will continue to surprise me. They'll do things I'll never be able to foresee, and I'll be watching everything they do and say very closely to see where they take me next.

I hope you're there with me when that happens!

Tom Dublin
May 30th 2018

PS - A HUGE thank you to both Tracey Byrnes and Randy Barber for allowing me to first write them into this story, and then bump them off in such a nasty manner. Being an author is both cool, and cruel!

PPS – MASSIVE THANKS to 'Tommy's Team' – Micky Cocker, James Caplan, Kelly O'Donnell and Erika Everest - the best damn beta readers in the world, for spotting my typos, keeping my stories straight, and politely laughing at the bits of the book I swear are funny and utterly refuse to see them any other way!

PPPS - I'm very excited to announce that I have a brand new, solo series launching this summer - 2018! It's all hush-hush at the moment but, trust me, you won't want to miss out!

To be first to find out more about this new series, hear about special offers and contests - and to receive a free comedy sci-fi short to get you in the mood - pop on over to www.tomdublin.com/free and sign up for my newsletter, *The Dublin Dispatch*.

AUTHOR NOTES - MICHAEL ANDERLE

JUNE 4, 2018

THANK You for not only reading this story, but reading our author notes as well. By now, I've written hundreds of these things—A good idea that has become a challenge as the company continues to expand and produce more and more books.

I'm not griping, just pointing out why I might not have as many things to say from book to book since between the last book in this series I've written another thirty author notes.

However, I want to talk a bit about Tom's humor. Specifically, I cracked up on the line "that we catch up with 007 when he's balls-deep in an ongoing mission."

Balls deep.

HAHAHAHAHAHAHHA...

I know, I've got a child-like sense of wonder right? Still laughing at what is equivalent to elementary schoolboy humor? I don't care, it's funny!

Tom says a few more things that I get to translate into

how he would talk. I might have mentioned it before that I met him in London in February 2018 and he's a small fellow with a big fellow's amount of humor.

(His best friend Barry Hutchinson is a big fellow with a big fellow's amount of humor but Tom has him beat in the humor per pound challenge.)

I've encountered the exact same thing Tom talks about when one of my characters in The Kurtherian Gambit did it to me. (General Lance Reynolds suddenly dropped to one knee to propose a whole book early. That rat-bastard stole my whole scene.)

I know I've been a part of a bunch of books, but I'm damn near positive I've never had to worry about passed-away spouses getting all chopped up to be feed to the poor.

Dark and twisted imagination indeed! Personally, I like his imagination as it is, and I'm happy to know he is working with us. (No, you other publishers, you can't have him. We have him, and we aim to keep him!)

If you have youngsters, I'd like to let you know that my collaborator has books out as Tommy Donbavand (Scream Street) for kids in middle-grades. He chose to use a new pen-name so those books wouldn't accidentally get mixed up with his work here in the Kurtherian Gambit.

You can find his work by clicking here: https://www.amazon.com/Tommy-Donbavand/e/B0029CUR3W/

We thank you for your enjoyment of reading, and choosing our stories to entertain yourself with… We don't promise you sleep, but we do promise to try hard to make you cheer for the characters, and want to re-read them again just so you can remember what they are up to and enjoy it a second time.

Even the new characters who come on board the book without permission.

Ad Aeternitatem,

Michael

www.ingramcontent.com/pod-product-compliance
Lightning Source LLC
Chambersburg PA
CBHW020413110726
47899CB00006B/1967